Also by Dasu Krishnamoorty

1947 Santoshabad Passenger and Other Stories

THE SEASIDE BRIDE AND OTHER STORIES

DASU KRISHNAMOORTY

ISBN: 978-0-578-21802-1 (sc)
ISBN: 978-0-578-21803-8 (e)

Library of Congress Control Number: 2019907099

Because of the dynamic nature of the Internet, any web addresses or links contained in this book may have changed since publication and may no longer be valid. The views expressed in this work are solely those of the author and do not necessarily reflect the views of the publisher, and the publisher hereby disclaims any responsibility for them.

Any people depicted in stock imagery provided by Getty Images are models, and such images are being used for illustrative purposes only.
Certain stock imagery © Getty Images.

IndiaWrites Publishers Inc.
66 Millbrook Road
New Vernon, NJ 07976
973-889-9220

Rev. date: 06/19/2019

To my family who inspired such happy memories.

CONTENTS

Confessions of a Writer

A Memorable Road Trip

PREFACE

My family has a history of migrations, the beginnings of which are traceable to my great-grandfather, a lawyer who left his village to test his fortunes in a big town. His son migrated to Bezwada to become a leading printer and publisher. His son, who is my father, migrated to Hyderabad, which at that time was geographically a part of the Indian mainland but considered itself a landlocked independent kingdom. When my father migrated from Bezwada with my mother and my three siblings, it was to recover from a deep hurt inflicted by familial discord.

I followed the precedent of my ancestors and notched four migrations in my life of ninety-two winters, at which point I began to wonder whether I could make a fresh move to uncharted pastures. *If that is not possible*, I thought, *I should at least pass on to succeeding generations glimpses of my experiences registered during my itinerant life in a world that was in an endless flux.*

By reminiscing and committing my memories to writing, I hope that the past I remember will enrich the present of those who come after me. Memoirs are a tribute to the past, an act of redemption by the present. Those who mock the past unknowingly disown their ancestry, their heritage, indeed their very parentage. Migrations find prominent mention in this volume because they occupied a large space of my past. Every migration is the story of roots and identity.

The semantic ruckus about the word *migrant* notwithstanding, I have used the word to mean a person who moves from one place to another within his country and have used *immigrant* to mean a person entering a country that is not his, intending to live there.

Migrations have not always been voluntary. By the time history began to be written, adventurers, in search first of legendary wealth in the Orient and subsequently power, sailed across the seas, invading countries and communities and destroying ancient cultures and civilizations of the East. In our own time, the partition of the Indian subcontinent witnessed mass migrations and massacres of people fleeing certain death, rape of millions of women, and upheavals of every area of public life. Hostilities between Indians and Pakistanis continue despite this history of fratricide. If people forget this slice of history, they will have no history to remember.

It is now the age of voluntary immigrations, again, on a mass scale, most of them from poor countries to rich countries, fleeing poverty, unemployment, religious and political persecution. Voluntary migrations are as large as the forced influx of slave labor of a bygone age, as evidenced by the migration of thousands of Indian engineers, doctors, and scientists.

For me, migrations are a device to frame my episodes because they happened during my evolution into a different person, taking in new experiences and new cultures, bonding with new people, breathing new air, and discovering a world that migration has made possible. Migrations also bring heartaches, the pain of separation, sometimes to a point of no return. It makes me sad to have lost friends and relatives, and along with them a sense of belonging, in my migrations. Yet there is a lot to be happy about in the memories they invoke—memories that resurrect images of carefree days spent with siblings and cousins, of adolescent love, of a life of amazement and happy incomprehension. Here they are.

ACKNOWLEDGMENTS

This volume would not have been possible without the constant support of my daughter, Tamraparni, and son-in-law, Kumar, who acted as advisers throughout and spent long hours reading, collating, reconciling, editing, and polishing multiple versions.

I would like to thank my friends Dr. D. S. Rao, former editor of *Indian Literature*, Sahitya Akademi's bimonthly magazine, and Mr. Raghavendra Rao. V. Harnoor, former news editor at the *Indian Express* and news coordinator of *A.P. Times*, who read many of my stories and suggested ways to make them shine. Mr. Harnoor is also a life member of Kannada Sahitya Mandir and Kannada Natya Ranga and a content editor at Globarena Technologies, an e-learning company.

I am grateful to my extended family and friends for patiently reading snippets and reminiscences I sent their way, which eventually came together as stories in this collection.

An Introduction
in Six Parts

Born in Doubt

The two persons who were eyewitnesses to my birth on July 1, 1926, are now no more. The midwife who helped my mother deliver me died when I was sixteen. My mother, who released me from nine months of incarceration in her womb, passed away when I was sixty-four years old. Strictly speaking, I should be the third witness, but I voluntarily dropped myself out of reckoning because I was without the faculty of cognition at the time of birth.

When I was old enough to go to school, I pleaded with my mother to tell me why I was dark when my brother was fair. I remember my mother telling me I was born dark because I was Lord Krishna reborn. She showed me a picture of adolescent Krishna with a cow standing behind him and a flute in his hands. I believed her because the boy in the picture also was dark.

In the middle of my school years, my mother thought it was time I heard the full story of my birth. On that day in the monsoon month of Aashadh, something happened that hastened my birth. According to her account, a few hours before my incarnation, she happened to enter the bathroom for an evening wash. She found an intruder in the bathroom, which in those days was built away from the main house. She panicked and ran into the main building. Immediately the labor pains began, the midwife was sent for, and that evening I was born, earlier than God had proposed, in an unused room of my grandfather's house. This account of my mother remains uncorroborated.

In their excitement that the founder of Dwapara Era was born to them, my parents had failed to register my birth with the Registrar of Births and Deaths. This omission wrote a prologue of doubt to my life. There was no document to show I was even born. The consequences began by stages to unfold.

In my fifth year, an orderly in my father's printing press took me to a neighborhood school. He introduced me to the class teacher as the son of my father. "That's great. What is his name?" the teacher asked the assistant.

Whenever I remember that day, I doubt whether my father's minion gave my real name to the teacher. "I don't know. But his parents call him Kishtu at home," he said. The teacher guessed "Krishnamoorty" and entered that name as such in the register.

Later, my mother told me that Sri Krishna was my correct name. But the Krishnamoorty moniker stuck to me like an election poster to a wall. That was not the end of the tragicomic tale. There were also doubts about the date of my birth. If I was born, as many people and I believe I was, it must have been on some day in the calendar. My school-leaving document showed it as the first day of July. But when my mother and I consulted the equivalent day in the Hindu calendar for Bahula Dasami of Aashaadh, the day of my birth—according to the family priest—was August 6 in the Christian calendar.

Throughout the world, the school document is conclusive proof of date of birth, which in my case was July 1. This duality of birth agrees fortunately with the Hindu belief that a Brahmin is born twice.

My life began in this manner with doubts, controversies, rumors, acrimony, and hearsay. Was it July 1 or August 6? Is my name Kishtu or Sri Krishna or Krishnamoorty? All these ninety-two years, I have been living with a name marred by ambiguity, regardless of the fact that school documents and later government registers accepted either of the two dates.

Evidence or no evidence, I had managed to get into and out of schools and colleges without a birth certificate. That happy run of serendipity ended one afternoon half a century later at the US consulate. What follows is embargoed information leaked for the benefit of impatient readers jumping the queue to know how the story ends.

My daughter, an expectant mother and an American citizen, invited my wife and me to come and help her. The next day, we showed up, visa-seeking, at the consulate. They asked me for my birth certificate. I asked the consulate official what more clinching proof of my birth was needed other than my physical presence before him.

"Sir, what we want is an official document testifying to the day, month, year, and place of your birth and the names of your parents," he said. And then he called the next person in line. *The end,* I told myself. I'd begun to doubt whether my existence was real or a trick of my consciousness.

The consulate official had no patience to listen to my metaphysical rigmarole. My wife, who got a visa because she had a birth certificate, was disheartened, but remembering something, she soon brightened up and said, "Why don't we try our luck at the Office of the Registrar of Births and Deaths? That might work. Who knows?" she said.

This unholy record of two mutually cancelling events of birth and death coexisting under the same roof had always intrigued me. But I remembered the Sanskrit saying that to be born is to die. Birth and death are made for each other. The minute you're born, you're headed for death. So, there is this umbilical cord binding birth to death, and the Office of the Registrar of Births and Deaths is a living confirmation of this truth.

My wife and I set out on a normal morning to the registry, asking people on the way for directions. "Near Kameswar & Co.," a person told us. "Proceed ahead for two hundred yards until you see, on your right, a shop selling old books. Next to that is the office you are looking for. It has no board. Ask the bookshop people. They'll help you."

We thanked him and moved on, remembering that as children we used to pass by Kameswar & Co. daily on our way to the branch of Sri Kanyaka Parameswari Vissamsetti Venkatratnam Hindu High School.

"Look! The bookshop," my wife cried in delight. We found ourselves in front of a complex of shops built on a ridge.

It was ten thirty when we climbed up five steps and reached a wide corridor closed by shop fronts on one side. At the bookshop, we checked with a small boy who looked like he was waiting for his boss to come take charge of the shop. "Next door. But *ayya garu* won't show up for another half hour," he said and pointed to a huge steel shutter covered with political graffiti calling for a

4

revolution. He said, "That is the office." Outwardly, it looked too poor to afford a name board. It sat between two shops in front of a building that sheltered out-of-towners for a small fee. One of the two shops sold bicycle tires, and the other traded in used books.

To kill time, we entered the bookshop. The twelve-year-old kid tried to help us, but my wife dismissed him as a presumptuous brat. "We will help ourselves," she said.

I thought we should buy a book or two and help the boy. After a half hour's browsing, I found, purely by accident, an old copy of Alexis Carrel's *Man the Unknown*. I tapped the book against a rack. It sprayed a cloud of fine dust, sending my wife into a paroxysm of sneezing. I read a few pages and found it hard to comprehend in a casual reading. The boy quoted hundred rupees for the book. Knowing the ways of traders, I said ten rupees. The boy said nothing. I didn't accept his silence as rejection and upped the offer to fifteen rupees.

"No," he said firmly. "He has come; talk to him," the boy said, pointing to the man who was just stepping inside.

The boy's boss, fortyish and looking harassed like Atlas bearing the celestial sphere on his shoulders, addressed us, "What can I do for you, sir?" He wore an overused sherwani, faded and frayed, secured in the front with discolored buttons. We told him about the book and the price we had offered to pay. He closed his eyes and did some mental calculations. After a few seconds of meditation and stemming with his tongue the ooze of pan juice from the corner of his mouth, he said, "That is not possible, sir."

"Make it twenty," I said. And then we tried to goad him by pretending to leave the shop.

"All right. Make it thirty, sir," he said.

"Final offer. Make it twenty-five," my wife said.

"Okay, sir, as you please. You are our old customer," he said, though we had never visited the shop.

As we exited with the trophy, we heard only half of what he had said. "Crooks," my wife, who heard the other half, told me.

When we arrived at the registrar's next door, the officer in charge, who documents God's creation and destruction, had yet to come. Time seemed to have pressed the pause button. I thought I could nudge it into motion by opening the Carrel book but my wife prodded my side with her thumb to draw my attention to a janitor opening a giant Aligarh brass lock that secured the registrar's office. The janitor heaved the shutter up, revealing the office display board.

In order to be summoned first, we rushed inside the room that smelled of burnt wood and aging paper. Huge ledgers were stacked on wooden racks, and more were resting pell-mell all over the place. Near the only window the office had, we saw a pot of potable water resting on a deodar stool and an aluminum tumbler chained to one of the window bars. A cardboard placard stood against the pot, admonishing the public that the water was strictly for use by office staff. A table and a chair for the officer and two more chairs across the table, for visitors perhaps, were the other pieces of furniture in the office.

The janitor began sweeping the floor and dusting the furniture, driving us out into the corridor. Ten minutes later, the janitor called us in and asked us to wait. My wife and I filled the time and talked about our smaller belongings that we could give away, in view of our migration, to servants and bigger items like furniture, the refrigerator, dining table and chairs, sofa set, TV, and others that could be sold to people in other flats. The biggest problem was the sale of the flat that the builder had built according to our specifications, floor-to-ceiling windows, washable paint for walls, customized doors, Godrej doorknobs and doorstops, mesh screens for doors that opened out on the corridor and the balcony and the windows, imported switches and switchboards, marble flooring in every room and on the balcony, and a score of other fittings not seen in other flats. These worries tormented us as we imagined the scenario that would present itself if our daughter asked us to stay with her permanently in the United States.

The janitor solemnly announced the sighting of his boss at the end of the corridor. In a minute, the boss entered the registry. We stood up and smiled at him. He wore a Binny cotton suit and took some time to settle down and call us.

"Birth or death?" was the first question he asked. He was a man of few words, clearly.

"Neither," I said brusquely.

"What else is the matter?" he asked us impatiently.

"Doubt," I said with a straight face.

"What doubt?" he snapped.

"The birth of a doubt, sir."

"Come to the point," the officer nearly shouted.

I told him the history of my undocumented birth and the unreasonable demand of the consulate official for a birth certificate.

"Sir, how old are you?" the official asked me. I told him my age. "They're gone, sir. It is impossible to keep such old records. After they attain the age of fifty, we destroy them. No chance," he said. We suggested ways of skirting the problem to him. That didn't work. We shook hands with him and stepped out, on to the Kameswar & Co. road.

As we neared Rajagopalachari's house, we heard a shrill shout from behind. "Sir, sir." We turned back and saw the janitor running up to us. "Don't be in such a hurry, sir. We can work out a way to get the document."

"How?" we asked him.

"Leave the how to me, sir. It will cost you something by way of processing charges."

"How much?" we asked him.

"Five hundred," he said.

I looked at my wife. She nodded. We went back to the office. The officer smiled at us in pity and in less than fifteen minutes issued us a certificate. I was born—a third time.

Bezwada: The Beginning

Bezwada was where all my siblings and I were born. We regarded it as our home from the time we were born, though we did not know how we came to be there until a friend of the family sent us a reprint of the three-column obituary that had appeared in *Andhra Patrika,* dated September 24, 1934, on my grandfather's death. The obituary said that my grandfather and a cousin fled home from Dokiparru to live in Bezwada. That was how the founder of our branch of the Dasus authored the family's first immigration to Bezwada, now known as Vijayawada, where I not only was born but went to school and college.

My earliest memories are of an environment of affluence and euphoria. My grandfather, a pioneer printer, had built a private powerhouse of his own to illuminate his twenty-one-room house and printing plant. The municipal power plant came much later. Passersby stopped and stared at his residence at night, an *Arabian Nights* spectacle. It was in this masonry sprawl that I grew up and my school days began.

The big village my grandfather had entered in search of greener pastures had now become a small town of great literary, political, and commercial importance, thanks to it being the railway gateway to the south and its status as the granary of the south.

The town boasted of every gift of nature—hills, a major river, and several canals branching off from it and flowing through the heart of the town. It was still evolving when the railway station hastened its urban march, with its interminable platform, shunting yards, and goods shed. It cleaved through the breadth of the town, bisecting it into western and eastern sectors like Berlin after the Second World War. The western sector is known as the town's business district, peopled by wholesale merchants, their lives focused on material success. The eastern sector known as Governorpet, where my grandfather lived with his three sons and their families, breathed a different culture created by doctors, advocates, engineers, teachers, and middle-level and senior bureaucrats. The big town is perched on the northern bank of the River Krishna. An irrigation canal starting from the southern bank of the Krishna passes under a bridge where the railway line cuts through the town and a few feet later trifurcates the Krishna Canal into Bandar, Ryves and Eluru canals, all three flowing through the town, investing it with a Venetian aura.

For us, the railway station was a great source of entertainment. It was on our way to school, but if we stopped to look, we would miss a class or would be late. So, we stopped on our way back. That was also the time when the Grand Trunk Express would arrive on its way to New Delhi. We would stop over a footbridge of the railway station and watch the steel locomotive hauling the Express majestically enter Bezwada Railway station, a matter of personal pride for us. The locomotives had names like Ganges and Godavari. The rest of the walk home would be filled with praise of the Express in superlative terms. The later Canadian engines lacked their majesty.

Our school, compressed in a private building, had no playground. So, outside school hours we would play in the open spaces of my grandfather's mansion where lived his three sons and their thirteen children. It was built on a sprawling square plot enclosed by four roads and consisted of the big house we talked about earlier, the cavernous hangar swallowing rows of composing racks, treadles, flatbed machines, a rotary printing giant, a power-house, an administrative complex away from the monstrous hangar, a typecasting foundry, and a godown to store newsprint and sundry printing stationery.

We really didn't know where the money came from. But as children, we had heard many tales about my grandfather's spirit of adventure that made him what he was, an uncrowned first citizen of the town, possessing two of the eight cars on its roads, with a double garage to house them. One was a Chevrolet; the other was a Citroen, both convertibles. The Citroen had solid tires and a chain, instead of a shaft, that connected the machine to the rear wheels. We sometimes sat in the driver's seat and, turning the steering wheel this way and that, pretended we were driving the car, all the time honking the horn to warn imaginary pedestrians.

The house is entered through a spacious vestibule opening out into a larger veranda leading to living rooms on the ground floor. The vestibule is flanked by two paved, open spaces where my cousins, siblings, and I played hopscotch and *gilli danda*. The girls were always spoilsports and quarrelsome. In the other open spaces in the printing complex, we played marbles. Since there was little traffic on the road opposite the house, we sometimes played football with a tennis ball.

In the evening, two bullock carts made the rounds of the town, playing pipes and drums. They distributed handbills of the films playing in the two cinema halls in the town, Durga Kala Mandiram and Maruti Cinema. We ran after the carts, collecting as many bills as possible. The one who collected most was envied. One day, an enterprising film distributor hired a trainer aircraft to shower the bills from the sky. The bills floated in air for some time before landing on treetops, roofs of houses, and the streets, with boys running helter-skelter because the descending bills lured them to one spot but actually landed elsewhere.

Fans buying tickets would mob the ticket counters hours in advance because there was no concept of queues in those days. One had to wrestle one's way through the pulling and pushing mob to reach the box office. Another struggle ensued to get out of the crowd, clutching tickets in your fist as if they were your very life. Those who failed to get tickets would wreak their frustration by throwing stones on the tin roof of the cinema hall. In the interval, spectators came out and sprayed the outer wall of the hall with urine.

We had always watched films in the company of our parents. One day, my father brought a small projector. With it came a few hundred feet of film. There was no soundtrack. The machine had to be cranked by hand. The film featured bandits raiding a town with guns, an action film. A special trick we enjoyed was to run the film backward. It was fun seeing horses race backward and shrug off the rider. Fire turned into smoke and reentered the muzzle of the pistol. My elder brother was the operator. Children of neighbors also craved to see the film. So, my siblings and I thought we'd start collecting gate money. When we became rich enough, we thought, we would build a cinema hall and buy real projectors. After some time, the teeth of the cranking wheel broke, foiling our plans.

The following summer, a granduncle of ours told us that his grandson, who happened to be our first cousin, would be coming from Madras for summer vacation. He was three or four years older than us. Madras is a big city where people traveled in trams and suburban trains. Boys and girls went to schools where they learned to speak English. When the cousin arrived, he matched our idea of a Madras boy. He behaved more like an uncle than a cousin.

To our great excitement, he took some of us to a hotel, local speak for a restaurant. We sat in one of the many booths. We called for *upma* and *idli*. As children, we were forbidden to drink coffee or tea. The bill came to one rupee. Asking us to go out and wait for him, the Madras cousin moved to a different booth and ordered coffee. A different waiter billed him for one anna. After coffee, he paid one anna at the counter and walked out to join us. Later he collected one anna each from us. Thus, he earned thirteen annas, cheating us and the hotel.

Talking of cheating, I had a classmate who would tell me stories about miracles. According to one of them, you could get anything you wanted by subduing a spirit. "You mean the spirit can build a palace for me complete with fairies?" I asked him.

"Anything you wish," he said.

"How is that possible?"

"This is how," he said. "Go to the cremation ground. When you see a whirlwind, throw some salt into it. A spirit will materialize. Without fear, you pluck a hair from any part of its body and tie it safely to your belt. Now, the spirit becomes your slave. Ask anything. It is done instantly."

The following week two of my cousins and I stole salt from our kitchen and set out for the cremation ground. Though it was broad daylight, the silence and the sight of bodies burning frightened us. We ran after each gust of wind, poured some salt into the whirl. Nothing happened. Meanwhile, the keeper, who happened to be a former employee of my grandfather, recognized me and told my parents about it. A severe scolding ended our quest for miracles.

HYDERABAD: AND THE MUSIC PLAYED

I didn't join my parents and siblings on their train journey on a breezy March morning to Hyderabad because I had to participate in a youth camp in a far corner of the country. But from the unedited accounts my brothers later gave me, I could fabricate a picture of their travel to and arrival in what looked like a different country.

My parents and siblings had made the journey to Hyderabad, our first immigration destination, by a passenger train that stopped at every station, helping them excitedly write down the name of every station between Rayanapadu and Secunderabad, from where they took a shambling meter-gauge train to Kacheguda, a suburb of Hyderabad city.

The station was no match to our Bezwada railway station in either size, number of platforms, or number of transiting trains, they later told me, pride shining in their faces. Yet Kacheguda station was a marvel of eye-catching architectural majesty and elegance. A fusion of Indo-Saracenic and Asafjahi schools. At the center of its roof was a clock tower with a dome that reminded you of the helmetlike headgear the Nizam used to wear. The station had a flourishing circular garden in front of it and a *tonga* (horse-drawn buggy) lot to its right and a customs house on its left.

Thus they landed in the territory of His Highness Rustam-i-Dauran, Arustu-i-Zaman, Wal Mamaluk, Asaf Jah VII, Muzaffar ul-Mamaluk, Nizam ul-Mulk, Nizam ud-Daula, Nawab Mir Sir Osman Ali Khan Siddqi Bahadur, Sipah Salar, Fateh Jang, the Nizam of Hyderabad, enough titles to crush a person under their weight.

Next to the tonga lot was an ordnance depot, a symbol of British hegemony. Today, this depot, the tonga lot, and the circular garden have their existence only in hearsay. A live steel locomotive resurrected from a bygone age and mounted on a circular cement platform in front of the station has met the same fate.

When I joined my parents and siblings after returning from the youth camp, I found people in this foreign capital spoke a different language and wore different clothes. All big buildings, including key government offices, were shrouded behind high walls, with an Arab armed guard in traditional garb sporting a half sword tied around his waist, sitting on a stool as a sentry at the entrance. They were known as Chaush, Arabs that the Nizams brought from Yemen. They were harmless people, we learned later, but pretended to scare children in jest.

When Mirza Ismail became the prime minister for a brief period, he pulled down the high walls of government offices and replaced the compound wall on Tank Bund that shut off view of the waterscape with a railing opening up the views to commoners. We were greatly interested in the cars of the Nizam's hospitality department known as Amera—the Rolls-Royces, the Bentleys, the Daimlers, the Humbers, the Rovers, Rileys, MGs, Wolselys, and so on. The unostentatious Nizam himself used an old-fashioned convertible for travel in the city.

My father had rented two flats, part of a four-flat apartment in Barkatpura, the best address in the city at that time, with the Nizam's ministers and secretaries as our neighbors. In front of it was a beautiful circular garden doubling as a traffic island, called *chaman* in Urdu. The very residence of these dignitaries assured security for the entire district.

The kingdom with its own postal system, its own railway and road networks, and an efficient public sector was the envy of the British-ruled region. In his dominion, the Nizam had the giant Singareni coal mine, the Bodhan Sugar Factory, Sirpur Paper Mills, Sirpur Silk Factory and Praga Tools, the big Nizamsagar project, and several small dams built across the Musi. The kingdom also had its own mint, an efficient road transport administration, and the public gardens in the city with a zoo attached to it. Under the Nizam, the city had the highest miles of cement roads in the country.

The kingdom had its own citizenship identity, called Mulki, and an Islamic calendar with Friday as the weekend. Education in Urdu, from primary to university levels, made the kingdom a real island. The language polarized the people into those speaking Mehmood-style Urdu and those speaking the language of Anjuman e Taraqui Urdu. It also built a wall around Urdu graduates who couldn't get a job or college seat outside Hyderabad.

Our acculturation began with buying a copy of *Bolta Khaida*, an Urdu primer, and practicing the script by reading display boards. We also began wearing pajamas at home and using flip-flops inside the house. We started listening to Hindustani classical music, soon graduating to host *mehfils*. When we entered the Islamic kingdom of Hyderabad, I remembered my grandfather warning me about the Islamic injunction against music even though the nawabs patronized music. So, at the customs in Hyderabad, I didn't mention my music background. You see, in Bezwada, as my sister learned music from Mangalampalli Pattabhiramayya *garu*, I sat by her side and listened to music from the basics to *kritis* and gained the skill of composing notations. Later, my sister joined us at Hyderabad to learn Hindustani music. Again, I sat by her side every day and listened to the melodies of *vilambit*. This was the beginning of my romance with music.

Freshly arrived peregrines, we set out to explore the geographic and historical landmarks of the city. On a Sunday morning, my uncle hired a tonga to see the great Charminar, famous for cigarettes named after it, sole competitor to W.D. & H.O. Wills. A pack of ten cigarettes cost one anna outside, but at Charminar, you got sixteen cigarettes for one anna. We rode through wide roads and a river of bicycles. Getting out of the tonga, we stood dwarfed and awestruck before the magnificent edifice, a civil engineering marvel of the fifteenth century, the city sentinel, a mute spectator to royal romance, court conspiracies, calamities like the 1908 floods and the recurring plague epidemic, and, most important of all, the seismic power upheaval in 1948 that ended an era of Asafjahi rule and inaugurated a democratic regime. This jewel of Hyderabad seemed to demand genuflection from spectators, architects, tourists, civil engineers, artists, and writers, from birds overflying it, pigeons fluttering around it singing its paeans, from historians, and from everything that called itself human.

Hyderabad is a city where history is impounded like it is in Delhi. Every graybeard living south of the Musi River has a swatch of history passed on to him by a grayer forebear.

Hyderabad was also where I found my calling. Thanks to my father's indulgence, I had dropped out of courses midstream at least twice. One such midstream change brought me to the bilingual town of Belgaum, a part of Maharashtra in 1945. I took an East-West meter-gauge train linking Machilipatnam in the East to Castle Rock in the West, from where another train took me to Goa in the Portuguese territory. When I arrived at Belgaum in the evening, it had just stopped raining. The platform was slushy. I came out of the station and found that tonga was the only means of transport. I told the driver to take me to the Law College, a well-known landmark.

It was dark, nearly time for supper, when I reached the college. I enrolled myself and entered a hostel room. I slept without supper. Next morning, I woke up to see that the rain had stopped and the sun was shining on the raindrops on the leaves of the trees. The district was known as Thalakwadi, a beautiful, middle-class colony of single-storied buildings, each of which had a moderate front garden fenced off by well-clipped boxwood hedges.

After obtaining a law degree, I never bothered to look for a job. This state of leisure continued for a long time when the government called for applications for several vacancies of assistant public prosecutors. My father asked me to send in my application. I could find no way to dodge. They called me for a preliminary interview. I gave deliberately indifferent answers at the interview to avoid selection. I was called for a second interview. Again, I performed wantonly poorly. In less than a week, an appointment order came by mail.

Around this time, a foreigner appeared, soaking in the rain across the public garden in front of our house. My father asked me to invite the stranger to take shelter in our home. I ran across the garden with an umbrella and brought him into the warmth of our living room. He told my father that he came to the city to launch the first university course in journalism at the Osmania University. My father, who in his time was also a journalist, permitted me to seek admission. That was how I escaped becoming a prosecutor.

Amdavad and New Delhi: The Best of Times

Before my wife, my daughter, and I migrated to Delhi, we moved to Ahmedabad (Amdavad to the locals) with the intent of living there after I was offered a position at a national daily newspaper. But we stayed there for only seven months following a breach of promise by my employer. We found the cityscape more modern than that of Delhi, despite some similarities. The two cities were colonized by both the British and the Moghul rulers. Ahmedabad is called the home of architects, and its residential buildings are a testimony to their architectural talent. Near Naranpura where we lived is a Mahadev temple that is a perfect specimen of modern architecture.

The people are extremely polite and friendly. All that appeared in the English press about Gujarat riots is fiction. My wife, who knew no Gujarati, English, or Hindi, traveled all by herself in the city without fear. My seven-year-old daughter went to a Gujarati school for four months. Our house owner's wife treated my wife like a daughter. But we didn't get to see any places of interest like, for example, the shaking minarets near the railway station or the Nal Sarovar. Not even Gandhiji's Sabarmati Ashram. Because our next migration was upon us. We saw only the Bhadra temple in downtown and the Mahadev temple in Naranpura. We remember fondly the vegetable bazaar where every vegetable is sold in five-kilo lots. Retail cart vendors give you ginger, green chilies, and coriander leaves free with every buy of vegetables. There is no count of the number of savories Gujaratis make with *besan* (chickpea flour), sold at every street corner on pushcarts, which we enjoyed every time we went out. When we were leaving for Delhi, many of the women in our street came out to bid us farewell. Though short, we remember our Ahmedabad sojourn for the affability of the Gujaratis.

I had to leave the job at Ahmedabad because a senior post that was promised to me went to a less qualified person, just because he had joined the newspaper a year before me. Learning of my frustration, a colleague of mine in Vijayawada told me that *Patriot*, another national daily, was looking for experienced journalists. Two letdowns from family-owned national dailies, one at Vijayawada and another at Ahmedabad, had forced on me yet another migration, this time to the country's capital. New Delhi was freshly coming to terms with a first woman prime minister who had impulsively split the Grand Old Party and showed the party's elders that she called the shots. The tumult in national politics plunged editorialists across the country into utter bewilderment. To accept the invitation of Edadata Narayan, editor of *Patriot*, a progressive daily that enjoyed an influence out of proportion to its modest circulation, I went from Ahmedabad to Delhi in April 1969, unaware of the ideological confusion gripping Bahadurshah Zafar Marg. Narayan's paper functioned from a building standing sentinel at the head of what Delhi pressmen pretentiously called the Fleet Street of India.

A meter-gauge express train from Ahmedabad, hauled by a locomotive resembling one of those Emmett creations appearing in the venerable *Punch*, brought me to Old Delhi station in the early hours of the first week of March, which marks winter's dying days in Delhi. A friend who was supposed to receive me at Old Delhi station failed to turn up. It was cold and dark, and I was a stranger to Delhi. Perhaps he was waiting for me at the New Delhi station, I thought. I took an auto. Its driver could have taken me round and round Delhi, honoring an old Delhi auto tradition of running up the meter. No, he delivered me honestly at New Delhi station.

I walked from one end of the platform to another twice, looking for my friend without success. Luckily, I had his Delhi address. It was a university hostel at Sapru House. I checked into a cheap hotel, backpackers' paradise, in Pahadganj, so that I could keep my bags there and go in search of Sapru House.

After a shower in biting cold water, I set out for the hostel in an auto. The driver brought me to the hostel just at sunrise. A janitor in the hostel was sweeping the corridors, softly crooning a romantic number from Saraswati Chandra. He took me to the room of my friend. In fact, it happened to be the room of a JNU student who had accommodated my friend for a week. He told me that my friend had shifted to Satnagar in West Delhi, but he kindly told me I could stay with him. I was delighted. I stayed with him for a week.

Patriot had its offices in the stateliest marble structure on Bahadur Shah Zafar Marg, the first building approached from the Tilak Bridge side and opposite the University Grants Commission building. I climbed up the very wide steps of Link House, the home of *Patriot* offices and its sophisticated printing press, walked through a corridor, and stopped at the reception, where a woman, plump and matronly, called the newsroom and informed the news chief of my arrival. After two minutes, she told me I could see him.

From the reception, I walked through a vestibule that ended at the door of the news chief's cabin. I could see the chief was a short man, though he was sitting before a large table, wearing a buttoned-down gray check shirt over a pair of baggy trousers. He told me to work at the desk for a week, producing the Dak (mail) edition. It was a sensible test of an interviewee's mettle.

As I entered the newsroom in flip-flops, carrying the burden of my forty-three years and small-town background, the copyeditors, all of them in their early twenties and some from preeminent institutions like St. Stephens and Presidency College, looked at me as if I were an anachronism. I took my seat at the head of the U table with arrogance disguised as confidence.

After the week was over, the news chief told me to meet the editor for a briefing on the paper and its philosophy. I met the editor in his large, brightly illuminated room. He sat behind a table as large as a billiards table. On the wall behind him was a painting by one of country's leading painters, Jagadish Swaminathan, who was the editor of the Hindi-language *Patriot*. When the editor stood up to shake hands with me, I found him tall, gaunt, and fair.

He told me in a leisurely manner that his paper was neither capitalist nor communist, two ideologies that fundamentally defined the policies of the Indian press. It was a different paper, he told me, before agreeing to let me join the paper's editorial desk. It was indeed different, with zero faith in the international press agencies' commitment to truth. The paper believed that these agencies used their accreditation to perpetuate third world stereotypes and propagate the Western views that supported, at that time, monarchies and dictatorships throughout the world. The editor had utter contempt for the capitalist press, calling it the jute press. He wrote a daily caricature of his critics called the

Fifth Column. As another eminent journalist wrote about him on his death, "Every word he wrote sizzled and burnt the paper on which he wrote."

My innings in the newspaper office began with an unexpected gift. There was a discrepancy in the pay the paper offered me. I protested. The editor told me that I could make extra money by writing for his daily and weekly called *Link*. That was how I began my writing career. My seniors at the desk envied me. I began writing every week on Latin America and gradually covered Africa and third world economies. Even though I didn't know who he was at that time, I wrote like Raymond Carver, using simple and short sentences.

Pending the arrival of my wife and daughter, I had roomed in Delhi with a friend in Karol Bagh. It was a large area, populated mainly by South Indians and Punjabi Sikhs and Hindus. It was a telling manifestation of North-South detente. The ugly caste politics in Tamil Nadu accounted for the influx from the South. From the North came victims of the Indo-Pak partition with just the clothes on their back. A common victimhood bonded both the communities, melded two civilizations and two cultures.

Delhi is a small part of the annals of the city ruled both by the Moghuls and the British. You cannot walk in the city without stumbling upon a piece of history every few feet—from Jama Masjid to Qutb Minar. Into this monument to history my wife and daughter arrived from Bezwada on the eve of winter with a baggage of language handicaps.

We set up a modest home in Hauz Khas, where my wife's pregnant sister lived. I had no idea about the social status of Hauz Khas until a colleague, on being told where I was staying, exclaimed,

"Oh, Hauz Khas—very posh area." The routine chores of grocery shopping, the early-morning trip to the milk booth, and dropping my daughter at school, where she met other mothers and Telugu women, sucked my wife and daughter into the giant melting pot of the city.

In the heart of New Delhi are around 275 villages, dominated by Raisina village, the home of Rashtrapati Bhavan. In the vicinity of Hauz Khas village are Shahpur Jat, Yousuf Sarai, Mod Munirka, Kalu Sarai, Katwaria Sarai, Ber Sarai, Begu Sarai ad infinitum. These are real villages where you see people lounging on string cots, inhaling hookah, and holding kangaroo courts. No city in India mirrors its cultural and demographic diversity as this ancient capital of the Pandavas. Delhi began to charm me, my wife, and our seven-year-old daughter. We found that living in Delhi was like living in a library. There are no books in this library. There are people; there are places; there are ruins; there is history, a civilization in constant flux; there are parties, politics, and processions, diplomacy and its paraphernalia, temples of culture and religion, *babas* and scandals, and a certain human species called *karamcharis*, who are everywhere like bacteria, with no work and all wages as their motto. To those who are alive to their environment, the history and geography of the twin cities of Old and New Delhi yield more knowledge than all their libraries.

We loved Delhi, where we lived for twenty years. A dining table we brought back from Delhi to Hyderabad evoked daily memories of Delhi and helped us relive some of our happiest days as immigrants.

America: A Writer
Is Born (Again)

There was no design in my becoming a migratory bird before I set foot on American soil as an immigrant seventeen years ago, my second-longest uninterrupted stay at any location. I had come to America several times in the past, always accompanied by my wife and always before winter showed its pallid face. This time I came not by a hurriedly fabricated Vietnamese boat or cooped in a Mexican truck trailer mounted on an eighteen-wheeler chassis but by an Alitalia flight with a four-hour halt at Milan on a Christmas day, bereaved and broken without my wife, who had died a fortnight earlier. My daughter and her husband who came to India for the last rites suggested I should move to the US and stay with them since there was no one in India to take care of me.

As we drove home from JFK, we passed through roads walled on both sides by mountains of snowdrift, dirty and brown at the base. We reached home as the darkness and silence enveloping the suburbia added to the gloom in my mind. We had dinner and went to bed. That night, my wife appeared in a dream and said, "So, you've come without me." I cried loudly and unabashedly, making my daughter and her husband rush to me and calm me down. The next morning, I woke up to a future of immigration I had neither invited nor intended. I found the house drowned in a bottomless pit of quietude. You could hear the sound of the earth circling the sun. But it was also the beginning of a most creative period of my life.

Seven years later, I became an American citizen. That day, I shed my old personality and acquired a new one, that of an emigrant. It was a weekday in April for those who are condemned to be young. Not for me, whose working days are a distant memory. It is five thirty in the morning. An American sun rises from the Atlantic, shakes off the saline water from his body, and gets going. He has my sympathy for his daylong east-west trek. In fact, he doesn't turn back and return to the Atlantic coast. He goes around the earth to get back to where he started. To be exact, he doesn't have a starting point or a destination. In my eyes, it is symbolic of the Hindu concept of birth-death cycle.

Sounds of morning chores in neighboring houses do not seep through the double-pane glass of my large bedroom window. The fragrance of freshly brewed coffee, the same old Lavazza, comes floating through the long corridor connecting me to the dining room and gently tickles my nostrils. I guess it is Kumar, my son-in-law, who has made coffee for himself and is ready to drive forty kilometers to New York.

I get ready to make what I can of the day before me. I emerge unwillingly from under the covers and amble to the bathroom to brush my teeth. That done, I am back in my room, where I switch on the computer to check the weather and mail. It is all junk mail, barring some pictures of my niece's newborn baby, who doesn't look any different from any other newborn.

But first things first. I go to the dining space where the coffee maker beckons. I make my cup of coffee and carry it to the computer table. As I made coffee, new mail had entered the in-box. Very bad, very sad. Prasad, my friend, student, and colleague, died of a heart attack in Stockholm. I am moved that his daughter remembered me at all, and in the midst of her grief, took the trouble to inform me. I mail this information to Prasad's other friends in Hyderabad.

I remember attending Prasad's wedding in Warangal and the frequent visits we made to the sandwich shop opposite St. George's Grammar School. Suddenly three beeps in my head tell me I have an interview at the immigration office that morning. My daughter walks in to say, "Naan, get ready with all the papers." She has abridged my address into a bakery item, the ever-popular naan bread served in Indian restaurants. I really hate to dress up, even if I need to become a US citizen.

We, my daughter and I, drive to the INS office in Newark, a metaphor for immigration. On the way, I try to guess what kind of questions I might be asked. Maybe I will be asked to recite the names of ten states, maybe the capital of Idaho or the name of the last president to be assassinated. "What were you asked?" I ask my daughter.

"That was many years ago. I don't remember," she says.

We are now before the INS office in Newark. We check at the front office and sprint to the immigration hall like all other new arrivals. The hall is already full, and applicants are being summoned. We have hardly taken our seats when my name is called. I raise my hand and wait for the usher to come and lead me to the interview kiosk. My daughter seeks permission to be present at the interview. It is granted.

"Good morning," I greet the officer in the cramped kiosk and sit in the chair facing him.

"Do you know English?" is his first question.

"That's English I have been speaking to you so far," I tell him.

Since my daughter has accompanied me, he surmises I don't know English. He asks me to tell the date of my birth, my mother's name, and place of my birth. I give him the information he needs and at the end add, "Anyway, they are all there in your files."

The officer thinks he has offended me by asking that question. He is ruffled but doesn't show it. He gathers himself and, stressing each word, says, "Sir, I am trying to help you, kindly understand."

If I can read the mind of my daughter, she must be thinking, *Father dear has messed up.* It is a short and brusque interview, at the end of which the officer asks us to wait in the hall and says that he will call us again. An hour later, he beckons us over the heads of other people who are waiting to be called. We go to him with apprehension.

He says, "Sir, we need bust-size photographs. In the neighborhood, there is a studio run by an Indian." He gives us directions. That is the first clue, I think, that my application for citizenship has been cleared. Happy, we reach the studio in a slum-like area. The photos are ready in fifteen minutes. We return to our seats in the hall.

Around late afternoon, a different official asks those whose applications have been cleared to follow him to a smaller hall. After a short briefing, he distributes provisional certificates attesting that we have become US citizens. The national anthem plays, indicating the end of the day and the beginning of a new life for me. My old self has disappeared. I am an American citizen henceforth.

The United States, where I am living now, venue of my last migration and creativity, is a multicultural country, an open society sheltering people from all over the world, and the world's biggest economy and military power. It has embraced me.

OLD AGE

People are afraid of old age because it is the penultimate stage. Next is darkness, the end, Hades. Old age is not terminal illness or a cardinal crime. It is a state of mind. It is a natural process not to be dreaded. The real old are those who have stopped thinking. For that matter, death doesn't spare the young either. If you know these immortal truths, you will enjoy old age.

Old age is also a time to relive the past, merely by reminiscing. Our family lost an empire. We didn't wallow in self-pity. We remember the past and feel happy that we were part of the empire once, and that we rebuilt ourselves.

At ninety-three, I use the computer for a minimum of eight hours, mostly mining Google, which is my dictionary, my encyclopedia, my pharmacopeia, and indeed my cornucopia. I compare it to Krishna's mouth containing the universe. From Google, I learned the dialogue between Yama, Lord of Death, and the young Nachiketa. Google will tell you how many versions of Ramayana are in vogue. Knowing that they too become old, the young will do better to plan and prepare for the rainy day. Age is how we manage it. I do everything I have been doing. Proof? The stories you are about to read, all of them written after my eighty-fifth year on this earth.

STORIES

CRACKING INFINITY

It is about infinity of time made more infinite by the silence of the primeval forest, as Kafka would have said were he alive. It hardly matters whether it is linear or cyclical. I am living in a house in the American suburbia after the death of my wife, which forced migration on me. I live in my daughter's house, made of wood and glass. It's a golden cage in which my fellow prisoner is infinity. My problem is different from what Ramanujan, the man who knew infinity, set about to crack in London. My problem is how to hasten the pace of time.

It is a beautiful house, one that John Keats would have loved to inhabit. It has the infrastructure to inspire romantic poetry. But wait. Infrastructure is such an ugly and unmusical word that Keats would never have stepped into such an unglamorous place polluted by the sound of that abominable word. Yet it is a lovely house if Keats pardons my inappropriate terminology.

It has six bedrooms, five and a half bathrooms, a living room, a family room as commodious as the inside of a mini theater, a kitchen resembling a Punjabi langar, and a library where the spirits of symbolist D. H. Lawrence and minimalist Raymond Carver clink glasses of champagne with John Cheever. There is also Virginia Woolf writing irreverent prose. The house sits on a mount in the middle of four acres of gardens and woods. Not far from the mount flows, unobtrusively, a small brook gurgling aquatic melodies in the shade of the soaring pines in a bid, perhaps, to lure Keats. Keats would certainly love to luxuriate in "the sensation of water."

In this house, originally built for writers of poetry, I lead a Saharan life. I scribble prose bereft of style and substance. The inside and the outside of the house meld like water and milk, benefitting from the transparency glass walls create. Others who inhabit the house are M. F. Hussain's unharnessed horses, Francis Newton Souza's hungry and dying humanity, and Laxma Gowd's Telangana peasantry. There are also Jogen Chowdhury's reclining feminine anatomies too delicate to stand the touch of a garment. One of Hussain's horses has two heads, eight fewer than Ravana. The unrealness of reality. Who used this phrase? I don't know. If the phrase suggests plagiarism, it is not my fault.

There is a gym in the house where you can happily sweat to grow unwanted muscle and look ugly. When it comes to flowers in the gardens, I remember Thomas Gray's lines about flowers wasting their fragrance on desert air. The scent of the flowers in the garden is too delicate to penetrate the glass walls. It is not the scent but the spectacle that coaxes me to write. I can see only the flowers closer to the glass wall because my glaucoma eyes refuse to see outside a twenty-foot radius.

I see lilies with six petals, each a color purple at the base that pales off into white. Right of the lilies are intensely pink wave petunias in clusters of long, thin tubes with flattened openings. I also see lantana florets clannishly huddled together in pink and yellow inverted cones. There are foxgloves too.

Beyond the ridge on which these flowers coexist exemplarily are peonies and hydrangeas, which even good eyes fail to see from where I'm viewing this floral extravaganza. Suddenly I see a gold-finch come hopping onto the ridge and begin to warble a melody, "Chip, chip, chipsy." What a pretty bird in bright lemon-yellow, black, and white habiliment! Sometimes I see them bouncing near the swimming pool, a delightful place where people sit around, forgetting to swim.

Ah, the endlessness of time in this house. It is a ranch house. It is six o'clock in the house of wood and glass. My daughter emerges from her room like the sun from the east. In her wake comes the evidence of habitation in the house. She finds me making coffee. I put three tablespoonfuls of Lavazza coffee into the filter. It was Folgers earlier. You need to put more coffee if it is Lavazza. But how much more I've no idea. I just take a chance and make it three. Now, the fragrance of brewing coffee and the auk-like gur-gle of the coffee maker awaken my son-in-law. The scent of fresh coffee spreads like a wild rumor to other parts of the sprawling glass cage and stays trapped.

With coffee in his hand, my son-in-law wakes up his school-going son. Then begins a fast-motion Chaplinesque pantomime, all the three characters of the family trying to squeeze more minutes from the hour. Suddenly, the garage door groans in the manner of a goat on its way to the abattoir. The labor of ascent, I suppose. For my son-in-law, it means the beginning of a thirty-mile cruise to his workplace. It also means the beginning of an evacuation of the house, my grandson to Allen Roberts Elementary, my daugh-ter to Florham Park. In ten minutes, all of them vanish, leaving a bottomless silence to rule; metaphor stolen from Albert Camus.

Seven o'clock now. I'm the master of all I survey (who said it?) through the transparency of the glass walls. First, I try to overcome the sullenness that envelops me after the flight of the threesome to different destinations. The problem of surviving the infinity of time challenges my resourcefulness. How to harness this cosmic phenomenon? Look at the grass, the plants, and the trees and feast on them with an eye on writing some pedestrian prose? Forget breakfast, you mean? The best thing, my inner voice tells me, is to break time into manageable segments and fill them with time-consuming activity.

Wait. If you create segments, you have to give each a number and determine what time it takes to fill each segment. On second thought, I defer the decision, choosing to act after I consult the man who knew infinity. Ramanujan? Is he also the inventor of time? No, sir. Time was there before anything and has witnessed the invention of God and His universe, His wicked ways.

I begin to peck at my brain with the fury of a woodpecker (1,200 times in a minute). To solve the problem of time, rather its infinity, I end up drilling a hole in my brain. But why do you need a brain? A starfish lives without it for thirty-five years. But I am not fish of any sort. In spite of the hole I pecked into my brain, it has not stopped functioning. Haven't you noticed that the information about the hole in the brain came to me from a functioning brain? I'm glad I've killed some time in manufacturing this rigmarole about the brain and in simulating cerebration untainted by purpose. But I've pushed time only by one hour. There are still four hours for the first of the three fugitives to return.

I walk up to the langar, the kitchen. It is not necessary to say kitchen every time because langar by any other name is langar. Open the fridge door. It has two. I look for time killers in the right door. Breakfast in slow motion will reduce infinity by one hour. Oatmeal or tomato sandwich? Let the mind linger on it for some time, or if you want an instant answer, you can search Google to know which of the two is more nutritious and time-consuming.

Google Uncle takes me for a ride, first to Grub Street in New York and then to a nutritionist who sings praise of a bodybuilding oatmeal sandwich. I haven't yet decided what breakfast I will make. Decide, you cretin, or clod if you prefer. Why go in for exotic things? Tomato sandwich is the known devil. Go for it.

From the fridge door, right if I remember right, I take out Pepperidge Farms white bread we bought at Costco. The whole world knows I don't like wheat bread. Spaghetti, for that matter. The other day, a TV crew attacked my house merely to ask me what dish I favored most. "Idli," I said.

"What is idli?" they asked. Stumped. On the net, I found a wise geek who gives clear answers to questions. Idli is a typical south Indian savory cake, he says, formed by steaming a fermented combination of rice and lentils. They are generally presented alongside sambar, curries, and other sauces. I gave this information to the TV crew, asking them to credit this info to the wise geek. The TV crew reduced my day by an hour. How I wish they came today also to ask about my views on weather. If you're keeping time, tell me how much time have I to kill before the first fugitive shows up, tired and hungry?

Suddenly, the aforesaid spaghetti transports me to its most celebrated worshipper, Haruki Murakami. I go to the library and find there three works by him: *1Q84, The Elephant Vanishes,* and *Blind Willow and Sleeping Woman.*

The first book is forbiddingly bulky and rules itself out. The other two are short story collections. I don't read novels for the same reason Raymond Carver hated to write them. When I open a short story book, I first see which story is the shortest. Now, let me choose one from his two collections. I toss a coin. It is heads. But I forget what heads stands for. So I keep the two books on the coffee table. I try to forget the titles so that I can be objective when I close my eyes and place one hand, right or left is immaterial, on one of the books. The book my hand happens to touch will be my choice. I close my eyes tightly. It doesn't work. I bring a towel and blindfold myself to rule out chances of cheating. Determined not to cheat, I place my hand on one book. I open my eyes. It is *Blind Willow and Sleeping Woman*.

Like a man who has dug his own grave, I open the book, go to "Contents," and begin counting the pages each story has claimed. My idea is to go for the shortest story. "A Perfect Day for Kangaroos" has that virtue. No, I'm sorry, I can't read it. There is already a kangaroo story in the other collection. He is crazy, I mean Murakami. He loves spaghetti, loves beer, and now loves kangaroos. "No way I'll read you, Murakami," I tell him. Why are they considering him for a Nobel Prize? God alone knows. Is God such a knowledgeable person? In that case, give the Nobel to Him. Wait, there is one reason I love Murakami. He loves music, mostly Western classical.

There is a lot of music in the ranch house. Classical music and music from films. I don't listen to film music unless it is vintage like *kahan ho tum zara awaz do* type. I throw the music plan out of the window because the music in the house is post-fifties. I suddenly remember Kumar Gandharv. We've plenty of his music in CDs. I go for a *Nirguni bhajan: sunta jaa guru gyani*. Gandharv takes off in his inimitable (I love this cliché from *The Dictionary of Indian Media Cliches*) folk style providing voice to Saint Kabir.

Kabir is saying and Gandharv is singing:

> Your soul has come from There to Here
> to quench the thirst for God.
> You unwise, you leave the nectar
> and drink poison again and again.
> Trapped Here you toss and turn
> to get back There.

Kabir then asks, "God, who am I?" God tells him, "You're I."

"No, it is I," says my grandson, the Allen Roberts brat, by ringing the doorbell and releasing such sonic violence that it chokes the voices of God, Kabir, and Gandharv in one foul stroke, so that the bell of his voice can be heard.

The infinity of time is cracked by a third-grade kid, my savior.

Journey's End

On an early-December morning, the mourning hoot of an owl awakens me, sending an inauspicious thought across my mind for a fraction of a second. Anyone in my place would have had such a thought. A valve in my wife's heart is leaking, say the doctors, and they are not sure whether either medication or surgery can fix it.

Now fully awake, I know what time it is without needing to look at the wall clock my cousin gave us when we moved in five years ago. Lazily composing itself, the velvety ambience of an early dawn pours through the large floor-to-ceiling window behind the headboard of the four-poster bed into the commodious living room of our new flat in Barkatpura, sailing the elevating strains of Kesrabai Kerkar's Lalit Gowri using both the *madhyams*.

Reluctant to roll out of the bed, I gently release myself from my wife's arm entwining my waist. Then I wait for her to make a movement that will assure me she is all right. A short wave of happiness courses through me as I find that the innocence and charm that captivated me when I first saw her at her parental home is still intact. But it hurts me that the transience of life is forever crossing her mind. I am afraid that such thoughts would disturb the rhythm of her heart. I exhale a sigh of relief when she tries to push back a wisp of hair bothering her brow.

In the temple next to the apartment, the priest begins a chant of Tulsi's Ram Charit Manas (Ramayana). From the *peepal* tree in the temple compound, *koels* (cuckoos) are raring to leave their perch in search of worms, insects, mice, grasshoppers, roaches, and other low life. For a minute, the relation between food, life, and death intrigues me. I come out of this brief philosophic reverie and hear the rebuilt vintage elevator which resembles an iron cage groan from the corridor outside, its labored ascent killing the quiet of the dawn.

The bells of the temple sitting next to the apartment launch a metallic harmony, indicating to the neighborhood it is *aarati* (homage to God) time. I hear again the mournful hooting, and it breaks through the usual racket birds make at that hour. With its pointed leaves, the peepal spreads a green canopy over the temple. Some birds take off noisily from the tree into the eastern horizon, later to separate from one another.

A new day, December 6, dawns. The sun, his face red with fury, readies himself from behind the Reddy Junior College for his westward trek. Time now for the up-and-down flow of milkmen, paperboys, maidservants, and flower vendors, orchestrated by the lachrymose creak of the wobbly iron cage, the hissing of rice cookers, and the cocktail of smells of lunches the stay-at-home wives cook for school-going kids and office-going husbands. The city, like the day, stretches itself, yawns, and gets going, with autos rattling up and down the YMCA Road.

I look up from the bedcovers my daughter left with us on her last visit. My eyes settle on the painting of the Lord of the Seven Hills above the doorway. My wife painted it when we lived in Delhi. It took her six months to achieve the gold and pink finish. She struggled hard to bring uniformity of impression to the pink tint. Involuntarily, I close my eyes, mumble a prayer to the Lord.

Wriggling out of the meditative web woven by the morning raga, I glide over to see whether my wife's heart is beating right. She lies calm and half-awake on the left side of the large bed, her head framed in a halo of her own luminescence. She looks like a saint waiting to be anointed. A nightgown with a print of tiny grass flowers encloses her wasting frame. Her body has begun to wear out. The doctors said that her heartbeat was arrhythmic but medication could set it right, and she placed herself in the care of the Heart Hospital, hoping to become what she had been a couple of years before.

We entered the flat on a February morning five years ago, without consulting the Hindu calendar, in the company of close relatives and a couple of friends.

My wife and I poured all our energy and emotion into imparting uniqueness to the flat, stamping it with our taste. The doors were custom-made; marble paved the floors; we designed the bath-rooms, filling them with the priciest ceramics. We persuaded the builder to fix windows larger than the ones he'd fitted in other flats. We quarreled over the color and texture of the drapes.

We wore ourselves out shopping for electric fittings, doorknobs, doorstops, granite counters, a stainless steel sink, and so forth. The walls received a paint that could be washed. With the elevator yet to be installed, we climbed up four floors every day to see the flat of our dreams reveal itself brick by brick.

At the housewarming, some guests remarked that the time of our entry was not auspicious. Those words did not reach us in the excitement of showing the guests around the house, still receiving finishing touches. Two hours into the flurry, we were all set to go out for lunch when she complained of breathlessness. Asking my nephew to take the invitees out, I stayed back to be by her side. The family doctor came that evening and gave a Deriphyllin shot. Much later, I realized this was the beginning of the end that was to come five years later.

She suddenly stirs in the bed to fend off the silvery strands dancing on her face. For a second, I recall images of her long dark tresses cascading down her back when I first saw her, a nineteen-year-old, at her father's place. The hair has turned gray now at sixty-three, but the glow of peace in her face stubbornly stays. Suddenly I remember for no reason the unfamiliar bird sound that stirred negative thoughts in me earlier. I feel anxious for her.

Entering the kitchen again, I set the water boiling for tea. The doctors have told her not to drink coffee. I reach for the tea and sugar containers when I hear the doorbell and next the thud of milk sachets dropping outside the doorstep. She has always hated that bell; when it rings, sets her heart palpitating. I open the front door, pick up the sachets, put them in the double-door refrigerator in the living room. She opens her eyes at the sound of the spoon swirling sugar in the tea. I bring the steaming tea to her bed, the same double bed I climbed out from before the sun rose. I pass the cup to her. With my cup in hand, I sit by her side. Her frailness moves me to tears.

"I love you," she says in her satin voice and caresses my head. That is an unusual declaration and gesture because she has never been overt in expressing love. She looks fondly into my eyes. She always used her smiling eyes to relay love.

"I know. But what's new about it?" I say, taking her anemic hand into mine and squeezing it gently to tell her, "I too love you."

"I don't know," she says.

"You perhaps thought I needed reiteration?"

"Nothing like that." She laughs wanly. The effort shakes her rib cage.

"You look better today," I tell her, believing such words will do her good.

"Don't tell me. I know everything," she says.

"Know what?" I manage to stifle a sob.

She quietly raises herself from the bed and walks slowly to the sofa by the large window opening out on the garden she'd raised three floors below. She peers down and cries joyously,

"Come! See what is there." She shows me the nosegays of golden-yellow, bell-shaped *suvarna ganneru* (yellow trumpet) flowers surging out of their serrated foliage. She has waited two years to see the tree blossom. "Don't they make life worth living in this lovely flat? You and I. No one else. My brother says in this flat I look like Empress Victoria in her marble palace," she says.

Her love of flowers mists my eyes. She raised a garden everywhere my job took us, Vijayawada, Ahmedabad, and Delhi.

"Did you open the mail?" she asks, her eyes glued to the suvarna ganneru glory.

"Let me finish tea first," I say. I cross over to the computer nestling in a Gauthier cabinet. I log in, printing her name for the password. "There is one mail from our daughter. Bobby says the doctors in the US think that the Indian diagnosis is correct. She asks us to email all the reports," I say.

"That's okay. Why don't you call the hospital? We've an appointment today," she says.

"I told you I'll call at nine when the secretary turns up for work," I say in a voice betraying impatience. At once, I realize I've annoyed her. The doctor is expected to tell us whether she can travel to New York. We have booked tickets to go to the US to stay permanently with our daughter because we need someone to look after us.

"Why don't you call your sister?" I say.

"I called her last evening. She is coming at nine," she says.

She then shuffles off to the bathroom, remembering she did not turn on the geyser. She comes back in and finds the day's newspapers at the doorstep. She collects them and slides back into the sofa. "Ayodhya, Ayodhya, Ayodhya! How long will this go on?" she hisses after reading a report that the opposition parties will move an adjournment motion. "There are no other issues. Poverty can wait. Women's reservation bill can wait. Everything can wait but Ayodhya and Babri masjid. There is really nothing else to read in the papers," she complains. Her comments on Indian journalism are interrupted by the silent arrival of the cook. She has come in early to make breakfast and to ask what we will have for lunch.

"What's the breakfast today, *Amma*?" the cook asks.

"What do you want?" my wife asks me.

"Idli," (steamed rice cake) I tell her.

"Oh, idli always." She winces as if idli were poison. "Let it be idli," she tells the cook in a defeated voice.

"What chutney?" asks the cook.

"The usual. Coconut," she tells her.

Breakfast was never our habit. We began eating breakfast after the doctors said that she couldn't take medicines on an empty stomach. The cook says breakfast is ready and lays the table. Before leaving, she asks what we'll have for lunch.

"Don't bother. Make a sabji (curry) and dal (lentils) of your choice," she tells the cook.

"Okay, I'll come back in an hour, amma," the cook says and leaves.

"We'll leave at nine thirty," I tell my wife at the breakfast table.

She looks lovingly at the laminated top of the table and says, "You know how old this is? Thirty years. We bought it from the Koorapatis."

"I know. Where are they now?"

"I've no idea," she says.

She remembers the appointment with the doctor and says, "Call the taxi guy."

"I've done it already," I say.

She puts three idlis in her plate and three in mine.

"Two are enough for me," I tell her.

"It won't hurt if you take one more," she says.

"No," I tell her.

"You're always like this," she says, her face showing her exasperation. What is wrong in accepting one more if that makes her happy? Often my sister and mother have chided me for lack of feeling. I always remember my obstinacy and repent after the event.

"My sister will be here any time now," she says and walks into her bedroom. I carry to her a glass of apple juice. Tropicana has just begun to sell in India. Earlier, I used to grate each apple and put the stuff in a cloth to squeeze the juice from it.

"I'll go shave now," I tell her.

"Listen, give this book to your cousin," she says.

"Don't worry, I'll do that."

We are disposing of things we do not need and have decided to sell bigger items of household goods. This book was set apart for my cousin.

I have never enjoyed shaving with a brush and soap and have long wanted to buy an electric shaver. I remember my father saying whoever invented the safety razor was a genius. I don't think so.

I begin soaping my chin when I hear a strange, bloodcurdling scream from my wife's quarter. It sounds like a grinder. I remember the unusual bird sound of the morning and fear that the worst is about to happen. With God on my mind, I reach her room in seconds. I find her unmoving on the bed. Her eyeballs are still, and the mouth is ajar. Despite a crippling shiver that creeps up my spine, I recover and look around for her Asthalin inhaler. I spray the drug into her open mouth, intending to clear her lungs of congestion. No response. I massage her chest hard, intensely hoping to revive it. Failure again. I fumble with mouth-to-mouth resuscitation. I sense a sudden blackout overtake me as if some light inside me has gone out. A feeling of unreality besieges me. Part of me refuses to believe what is before me. At that moment, I wish I were someone else. No, I remain the same: her husband, a widower, bereaved.

It doesn't take me much time to accept the irreversibility of death, the end of a forty-five-year-old marriage. Seventeen years later, I haven't pardoned myself for so readily accepting the reality of her absence. A distance already begins to spread between her and me. She is a body now, waiting for its fiery end. How could I disown her so swiftly?

Now, the cruel press of realities asserts itself. I pick up the phone and call her friend on the second floor. "Please come up at once," I tell her. My voice quivers.

"Just now?" she asks.

"Immediately," I say.

She comes up the next minute, before another friend of hers joins her. Both are stunned.

"How did it happen?" she asks.

"I've no idea. She didn't tell me," I say amid sobs.

She, teary-eyed, calls the family doctor who treated my wife after the first attack of asthma. Waiting for the doctor, she and her friend try massaging her heart. The doctor and her husband, also a doctor, arrive. He feels her pulse and loses no time to say she has died of asphyxia. His wife chides him for not bringing the nebulizer with him. He briskly writes a death certificate, and the couple leaves after a few words of sympathy.

I go over to the phone and call my cousin. His wife answers.

"Ask him to come at once."

"What happened?" she asks.

"She is gone," I tell her.

"What? Is she talking?"

"Nothing. Everything is over."

"We'll be there," she says and hangs up.

"Please call my daughter," I tell my neighbor.

I sit by my wife's body, grieving how she became a memory so suddenly. To preempt rigor mortis, I softly press down her eyelids and straighten her knees and hands. A doubt torments me. Was she struggling to say something with her eyes when I closed them? I give in to a sense of guilt and break down, sobbing, "Oh, you have left me without a word for me." I let out a muffled cry and slump in a nearby sofa.

Her sister comes in at nine twenty. Seeing my grief-stricken face, she asks, "What happened?"

"She's left us without saying a word. I do not know whether I've wronged her. She could have told me. Why should she keep it to herself?" I say, my voice too frequently faltering.

She goes into her sister's room and issues a pathetic cry, "Oh, Akkayya (elder sister), what have you done? Why did you leave us? Where is the hurry?"

The hall is now filling up with relatives, friends, and others coming in to commiserate. My cousin and his wife come first. All my brothers, their wives and children, my wife's sisters and their children, her cousins and mine, come and begin discussing what needs to be done next. My neighbor asks her husband to come at once. Someone asks whether anybody has called his daughter in America.

"Yes, I spoke to her. They're coming the day after tomorrow. She told us not to keep the body for her sake," says my neighbor.

Surprised, my cousin says, "How can that be? Let me talk to her."

He lifts the phone from its cradle to book a long distance call to the US. "Uncle here. Do you want us to keep the body for you to see? It'll be good if you have a last look at her ... All right, I understand." He hangs up, telling others, "She says she can't see her mother in that state. I understand her point."

It occurs to me that a lot of money will be needed. I open the Godrej almirah and see her clothes neatly folded and pressed and try to suppress a fresh wave of sobs. I find quite a lot of money, some in her purse, some in saree folds, and some in a small notebook. I give most of it to my neighbor for safekeeping. I hand over a few thousand rupees to my cousin, telling him, "Spend it wherever you need."

My wife's sisters and a niece help her body out of the bedroom and gently lay it on a mat in the hall for all to see. The niece covers the body up to its neck with a white sheet of cloth. Her elder sister brings a clay bowl, pours oil in it, and, making a wick out of a piece of cloth, lights it and places it at the head of the body. The womenfolk gather around the body. One of my wife's Delhi friends recalls the times they spent with her. She breaks down and hides her face in her palms. "What an active woman she was. Made us join the English classes," says another neighbor from Hauz Khas.

"Yes, I know. She enrolled us for music lessons," says another friend.

"She is lucky she died before him," one of them says. What could be lucky about her dying?

My neighbor's friend meanwhile brings tea in a big canister and a few paper cups. One of the girls volunteers to pass tea to the visitors. My young nephews and my cousin are busy assigning chores to themselves when two doctors from the L.V. Prasad Eye Institute silently walk in. I had no idea who called them but am happy to give her eyes away to the Eye Institute—my homage to her, to bring light into someone else's life. One of the several short stories my wife wrote concerned a poor boy regaining his sight after receiving eyes from an accident victim.

"We're very grateful for her gesture. Will you please fill this form and sign it?" The doctors reverently pass a sheaf of papers to me.

"I'll do that. First let me know whether you can do it without disfiguring her face."

"No, not at all," they say and explain in detail how it will be done.

They request everyone but one or two persons to leave the room. They finish the operation in ten minutes and ask those visiting whether they are willing to become donors as well. A few young people fill and sign the forms to donate their eyes. The doctors come back to me, thank me, and leave.

I am tired and flop on a sofa, the same sofa from which she had admired the yellow trumpets in bloom barely an hour ago. In that moment of grief, I remember many things in a rush. But time and again, I remember her love for her daughter and myself and how she cried uninhibitedly when our daughter was hospitalized for meningitis. How she assimilated in her heart my inadequacies and idiosyncrasies.

My younger brother and my wife's sisters sit around me, asking whether I need anything to drink.

"I don't want anything. Please tell me who will do the karma," I say. I know that the person doing it must be an orphan and related to me as a son or nephew. Sreedhar, one of my elder brother's sons, says he is ready to do it, despite his heavy schedule and a recent bereavement of his own.

It makes me happy to know everyone is with me in my grief.

Somebody rushes into the hall and says that the priests have come and suggested that the body be brought down to the ground floor. I try vainly to cushion the implosion of self-pity as my nephews lift and cradle their aunt's lifeless body, now lightened by death. They carry it down the staircase. I go down by the elevator and sit in a plastic chair beside her body to witness the melancholy rites of her last bath.

My neighbor's husband clears the parking lot of all vehicles and gets it swept and washed. The women rest her body against a pillar facing the south, and her sisters bring turmeric paste and swathe her smiling face with it. The aura lingers. Her elder sister spoons into her mouth the Ganga water Sreedhar brought from the temple next door. The others pour pots of water mixed with milk, curds, ghee, and sesame seeds on the body. A reflection of the garden she raised spreads on the water as it flows down her body. The priests chant hymns from the Purushasooktam.

A long ring comes in. My daughter from the US.

"Nanna (Father), we will be there day after tomorrow. Are you all right?"

"I'm okay, my child. Don't worry about me," I say, sobbing.

"Take heart, Appa (Father). We'll be there," her husband says.

The priests bring with them two long bamboo poles and four-teen short slats. One of them begins fabricating a ladderlike bier. The slats make the seven rungs of the ladder. The priests begin chanting at the body. When they finish the melodic chant, they ask the body to be placed on the bier. The priests ask my brothers and me to walk around the body three times and at the end press grains of rice into her mouth. The priests launch a fresh round of Rigvedic recitation. I do everything in a daze.

"The ambulance has come," cries my cousin as he spots the van entering the apartment complex. The nephews brace to carry the body into the vehicle but tarry to let the womenfolk who stayed on take a last look. They heave the body on to their shoulders amid emanations of subdued grief from the women. They roll the bier onto the aisle at the back of the truck. They get into the van and take seats on the benches flanking the aisle. Friends, close relatives, and other occupants of the flat get into their cars. I sit glumly in my neighbor's car.

The convoy leaves the gates of the apartment complex and after a short drive turns left into an alley where my wife and I lived for a few years before we came to the present flat. The motorcade progresses through Barkatpura, through scenes familiar to her—Delhi Sivamma's unoccupied lot, Tulja Bhavan, Kacheguda railway station—and veers right to enter the Nimboli Adda road. After a few minutes' drive, the cars take a left and shortly afterward wheel right through a gate and come to a halt at the Amberpet crematorium, familiar to me because fifty years ago I cremated the paralysis-stricken body of my father. The mourners pour out of the vehicles and silently enter a well-lit large hall and wait for the body to be brought in.

The body is borne into the hall. A *sardarji* (member of the Sikh community), keeper of the crematorium, asks the pallbearers to place the body in the middle of the hall. I, my nephews, other relatives, and friends from the flat stand around the body in a semicircle. The chief priest comes and starts a final round of last rites. He asks me to circle anticlockwise around the body because, he explains, everything is backward at the time of death. As I circle the body, I shift my sacred thread from the left shoulder to the right.

My cousin, who has studied Sanskrit, reads out this stanza from the Bhagavad Gita:

For certain is death for the born
And certain is birth for the dead;
Therefore over the inevitable
Thou shouldst not grieve.

On a signal from the priest, the sardarji opens the doors of the incinerator. The nephews lower the body gently into a casket. The casket is then placed on a roller-equipped pallet. The sardarji asks my nephew to remove jewelry or any gold on the body. Everything is now ready for the final act. All the mourners glue their eyes to the casket, anxious to take a last look before the body goes into the chamber of the incinerator, preheated to 1100 degrees Fahrenheit. In that last moment, she looked as fresh as the boat orchids she had grown with great effort on her balcony. As the casket slips into the cremation chamber, the doors close. The sardarji asks me to press the button, symbolic of the act of lighting the pyre. As I push the button, my heart beats wildly. I know men do not cry. But they are not husbands.

"She is beyond us now," somebody says. What remains are her ashes and memory. She has offered herself to Agni, the acceptor of sacrifice. From Brahman arose space, from space arose air, from air arose fire, from fire arose water, and from water arose earth. Swallowed by fire, her body, composed of the five elements, has now renounced them to let them return to their abode.

From now on, I can see her only in the family album or in a dream. She is now a chapter to be added to the next edition of the family annals. Tomorrow will dawn without her. Every night I am destined to go to sleep hoping she will appear in a dream.

Junking the Past

We sit on the bare marble floor, my wife and I, in our flat in HVS apartments, on the third floor. Each floor has a running corridor open on one side, turning the corridor into a long, balustraded walkway. Ours is the only flat that has a screen door. That helps strangers to spot it easily even if its number is fudged or masked for some reason. The screen door lets you into an L-shaped hallway. That is where we are sitting before a pile of declassified papers, diaries, electricity and telephone bills, ration card, photos that failed to get into the family album, notes, copies of articles submitted for publication, letters received, and things we do not know why they are there and what to do with.

The hallway is a point from where you can reach the kitchen and one of the bedrooms on the north and a bathroom you can enter from the hallway. West of the bathroom is another bedroom that has a bathroom attached to it. Barring the hallway and the kitchen, none of the other rooms is a player in this story. Clearing the pile concealing unedited history is a precondition to our immigration to the US. You'll learn the details as we proceed.

We can't carry all this garbage across the Atlantic. It's easy to appreciate our inability to carry if you know we've lived in this house for six years, filling it with a TV, a tape recorder, drawing room furniture, two beds, a double-door refrigerator, an air conditioner, kitchen gadgets, dining table for six, crockery and scores of gizmos, and a hundred other things we gathered to keep up with the Joneses. As a first jettisoning step, we gave away our larger belongings like furniture, refrigerator, and steel cupboards to whoever wanted to buy. Bed linen, many items of clothing, and electric appliances have gone to relatives and friends. The cook and the maidservant pounced on the kitchen utensils, the gas stove, and cylinders. I can picture the maidservant and her family celebrating the acquisitions with pooja to the double-burner stove and the cylinders, daubing them with turmeric and vermilion. The computer went at a throwaway price to a relative who has a high school–going daughter. What is the daughter doing now? Googling? My wife muses. No chance; there's a power cut now, she tells herself.

Don't ask me why we're wasting time wading through this mess. You won't ask if you knew I found in the heap a pamphlet of 1925 vintage. It was an invitation by my grandfather to his friends and relatives to attend a concert of Ustad Abdul Karim Khan he was hosting at his home. Who knows whether more such scraps of history will surface? But why those electricity, telephone, and house tax bills? you ask.

You must live in my country long enough to know the hazards of throwing those scraps away. Suddenly you may get a demand to pay an amount you already paid three years ago. If you fail to show the three-year-old yellowed receipt, you will have to pay a second time. Most of the paper junk before us belongs to this category. Not this Penguin-published *Saint Joan* by Bernard Shaw. How it fled its shelf and joined this unscholarly company I've no idea. It's a paperback priced at fifty cents in 1948 when I bought it from Swatantra Book Shop of Bhushan Rao in Sultan Bazaar.

I begin to run through the Shaw book and remember Ingrid Bergman as Joan and the dazzling spectacle Victor Fleming crafted from the French legend. My thoughts go back to the Plaza Theater, where a cousin of mine and I saw the film, and to our trek back five miles home because we'd missed the last bus.

My wife senses my migration to another world. She pats me on the back. "Where're you? At this rate, you'll take a week to do the job. Let's take a break and have some tea," my wife says, sizing up the pile, looking bored.

"Fantastic idea." I welcome her suggestion but never take my eyes off the Shaw book.

My wife jacks up her frail frame from the floor in slow motion, like the replay of a catch or fall of a wicket in cricket, and sets one foot in the kitchen, as a first step to making tea, when the telephone blares, making her heartbeat skip out of rhythm.

"Take that call," she shouts to me and enters the kitchen irritably.

"It's an overseas call from our daughter," I tell her.

"How are the preparations?" my daughter asks me in her foreign voice.

"Imagine the two of us battling with the contents of a two-bedroom house," I tell her, examining an old photograph that showed itself up from the heap a while ago.

"I'm sorry, Dad, I know it's a pain but it needs to be done. Why don't you ask your favorite nephew and others to help?" she asks.

"Why didn't you call me when our daughter is on the line?" my wife chides me as she rushes from the kitchen and wrests the phone from me. A glare from her deflates me.

"Yes, Bobby. What's the news?" she asks her after telling me to go mind the tea on the stove.

"Hundred years just to make tea," I complain to the detritus of the past looming before me.

"No news, Amma. Just wanted to know how you are coping with packing and other things," our daughter says.

"Everything is ready—the passports, the visas, and foreign exchange. We are waiting for the tickets," my wife says, looking through the window unfocusedly at the flame tree she planted three years ago that is now level with our living room window.

"The travel agent tells us you'll get them next week. Amma, there is an incoming call. I'll call you again in a day or two. Take care," our daughter says.

"Okay, my child," her mother says and puts the receiver back on the hook fixed to the wall and wonders what her darling daughter would be doing at that time.

My wife walks back to the kitchen and finds I had put the tealeaf in the boiling water. She empties three spoons of milk in it, adds sugar, and stirs the beverage. She returns with the tea and places my cup on the bare floor.

"Good," I declare, taking the first sip.

"Better than the rainwater you make," she says, dismissing me.

"Agreed," I say to end the run-in.

I then turn to examine the aging photograph that raised its head unasked from nowhere, a family photo taken in 1939 at Sundaram studios. Everyone in the picture except me is dead. Sundaram too, unless he is alive as a doddering survivor at 110 somewhere, sought after by media hounds. Though I was thirteen at that time, I don't now remember the trip we made to the studio, whether we walked down or hailed a *jutka* to the studio. But I remember the photographer struggling to fix the tripod, insert the plates in the camera, and dive his head under a black cloak. I don't think he said, "Steady, ready, smile." That may be why you don't see any smiling faces in the picture.

The Sundaram relic showed my father and mother sitting in the second of three rows, in two studio chairs worn down by previous patrons who perhaps came to refurbish their image that had lost its gloss like the picture of Dorian Gray. An old soiled cloth was hung behind us as a background. Or, was it some kind of a surrealistic mural? The floor was covered with a cotton carpet full of dust and odor I could not see or smell from the picture. Some of us were lined in a row behind my parents and others at their feet. I stood behind my father, holding the back of his chair lest it should suddenly cave in. My elder brother stood behind my mother's chair, looking bored and indifferent. His hands were off my mother's chair because he didn't know what to do with them. The story goes that in his first film, the famous actor Ashok Kumar didn't know what to do with his hands. The director gave him a cigarette to hold. My brother perhaps had a similar dilemma.

Between my elder brother and me stood my sister, newly married. She wore a white chiffon saree. She had a neutral expression, neither glum nor glad. She dropped her hands loosely by her side. You can't see them in the picture because she covered them with her *pallu.* My father sat stiffly with his hands in his lap, a posture popular with men of his generation facing a camera. He was dressed like a traditional Telugu *pater familias* in a white kurta and dhoti, an *uttareeyam* snaking around his neck and shoulder. Doe-eyed, my mother was unself-conscious. She was draped in a silk saree. I forget its color now. At the feet of my parents, my two brothers who were born after me sat cross-legged. The brother who followed me first into this world looked the brightest of all, his natural, contented self. The youngest tilted his head so much to his right that he seemed to ask the photographer whether that posture was okay.

At the time of the photo session, I was old enough to know the family was going through a bad period. Our family migrated to the Nizam's Dominions a few days after the photograph. My father's outfit was so simple and Indian that looking at the picture you'd not guess that he had studied law at Gray's Inn and had worked for the *London Times.* One of the several anecdotes he used to tell us about London was about his arrival at Tilbury Docks. He had to go to his uncle's place in the city. A cab pulled up outside the port. My father thought a cab was expensive and decided to take a victoria. When he reached my uncle's place, the uncle laughed and said, "You fool, the cab is cheaper." My father was full of such tales he entertained us with when we were children, I tell my wife.

"Look how beautiful your sister was when she was young," my wife says, standing behind me and examining the picture over my shoulder. I look at my sister's face fixedly like a hypnotist. Slowly,

I detect a smile forming on her lips. Her eyes brighten. Her face reminds me of the day I held her hand firmly to prevent her from yanking off the tube connecting her hand to the glucose drip. She was ill, and I could feel her temperature slaking and the body becoming cold. Life flowed out of her. I remember the last rites I performed and begin to sob silently.

It touches my wife. She places her consoling hand on my shoulder softly. "I know what she meant to you. She had told me how you sat by her side every evening during her ten years of learning music. Wasn't she the one who brought the two of us together? Die people must one day. We can't help it," she says and gently relieves me of the photograph lest I should remember the others in the picture and cry afresh. To divert my attention, she says, "How did you amass all this scrap?"

"I didn't do anything. It is in the nature of things to come together and pile up," I tell her. I grant asylum to many things—papers, books, trinkets, pictures, and memories. Eluding my oversight, some stuff smuggles itself in like illegal immigrants. I let these oddments of human caprice hibernate in whatever crevice they choose to hide. Preserving the past for the future!

Often these discards irritate my wife, who threatens to throw them away or throw me out. But she forgets she too does what I do, collect and preserve odds and bits and keep them in the museum of her kitchen. Neither of us catalogues the pile. We just let them be, in the humble belief that they become antiques with the passage of time. Every tick of time adds to the vintage of the oddments. The Midas touch of time.

I go back to the cupboard to discover sly junk that has escaped my casual eye. On the upper shelf serving informally as some kind of an old-age home for history, I find a bundle of yellowed and brittle letters secured with a rubber band that my wife uses to gather her aging hair. The film of dust that layers the bundle, certifying to its antiquity, makes me sneeze in rhythmic succession. *Portentous*, I think. My wife, an asthma patient, harangued me countless times for housing such geriatric stuff. As if I were housing evil intentions.

As soon as I open the dusty packet, I meet Dame Luck with the very first letter. My father wrote it to his uncle in Bezwada exactly a hundred years ago—the year of King George V's visit to India. I flourish the letter before my wife and say, "Look, the reward of hard labor!" A century ago, my father was a matriculation scholar at Allahabad. From there, he made a trip to Delhi to see the royal festivities and wrote a book, *My Delhi Durbar Trip*, copies of which used to lie around in his office when we were learning the English alphabet. We tried to get a copy of it, years after his death, from the Vetapalem and Rajahmundry libraries. No luck.

Let me tell you a silly story a friend of mine told me. It seems he found at his home a fading green, steel trunk that went to sleep when his grandfather died. He woke it up. Broke it open, perhaps. What he found first was the carcass of a rat. He persisted. From the debris of the past slipped out a sepia photograph of a sixteen-year-old drop-dead beauty. It was the picture of his friend's grandmother when she was not even a mother. He showed it to his children and said that she was their great-grandmother. All of them laughed their sides out and said what a joke. It occurred to him later that he should have told them it was his grandmother at sixteen.

Back to where I took a break: I thrust my hand farther into the heap to mine for things that eluded my reach. What I later discovered to be matters of the heart, an epistolary treasure, arrested the progress of my hand. Guess what it is! Letters my wife and I wrote to each other, thanks to brief spells of separation. Every time I had a new job away from my place, I would go first, look for a house, and then write to her to join me. Of course, the separation always ended with my renting a house.

Our letters were written in officialese on what were known as inland letters, the country's lowly postal stationery at that time. My wife talked mostly about the antics of my toddling daughter, how she refused to drink milk. How she eluded her eye and stepped out onto the busy road. I wrote about work at my new newspaper, whose late editions frequently used to miss trains and flights. In one letter, my wife mentioned *Brahmachari*, a Shammi Kapoor film she had seen in the company of a friend, and suggested that I see it in Ahmedabad, where I was employed at that time. In my reply, I told her I had seen it and it was a film she shouldn't miss. The letter amused her so much she told her friends about the tricks that memory played with me.

Luck refuses to desert me. I nearly forget why I am doing what I am doing. Yes, junking. Instead, I'm delving into the past and wondering at the joys memories bring. I haven't stopped wondering when two documents bob up, stoking a throwback to a colorful ceremony on the eve of our wedding. Our family, relatives, our friends, and we had swarmed the bride's seaside town a day before the wedding like devotees thronging Tirupati. We were to participate in a few premarital rites at my sister's place and the bride's house. Both houses were dressed up in festoons of green mango leaves and marigold flowers. At dawn, a small train of women from the bride's side called at my sister's house, temporarily converted into a lodge for the bridegroom's party. They'd brought breakfast for us, the groom's side. It's a tradition. The fare was the same as at every other wedding: idli, upma, coffee and a slice of the lemon to garnish upma. We were in the middle of breakfast when word came that our presence was sought at the bride's house. Hurriedly, we finished our breakfast. We went in a small procession and entered the courtyard of the bride's house, now covered by a canopy of green palm leaves. We sat on carpets spread on the verandah where I had seen the bride for the first time on a November evening. At a nod from the Brahmin priest conducting the ceremonies, the bride's eldest uncle began reading from a foolscap white paper: "Let there be wealth, welfare, and peace on this earth on the occasion of this invitation from Ramamoorty, uncle of the bride, to the family, relatives, and friends of Trivikram Rao, now residing at Hyderabad, and father of the bridegroom, to be present at the wedding of his niece Bharathi, second daughter of his youngest brother, now residing at Bapatla, with Trivikrama Rao's second son Krishnamoorty, decided by elders to be performed at the residence of his sister Varalakshamma in the early hours of Saturday, the second day of the first fortnight of the Magha month in the lunar year of Durmukhi at 4:55 and to shower their blessings on the bride and bridegroom and accept my humble hospitality and thus render me happy."

When Ramamoorty finished the recitation, Trivikrama Rao, my father, read out a similar invitation to the bride's side, followed by exchange of clothes and jewelry between the two families. Minutes after we returned to our lodge, the brother of the bride, accompanied by his father and close relatives, came over in a procession, carrying with him a pair of clogs, an umbrella, and a walking stick. I was already briefed on the part I should play in the theater that was to follow. At a hint from the priest, the bride's brother pleaded with me to marry his sister. I said I had no intention to do so because I was renouncing the world and would go to Kashi to live the rest of my life there as a hermit. The brother said, "Sir, I will wash your feet if that will appease you and make you accept the hand of my sister. Please wear these clogs, and with the help of the umbrella and the walking stick, you should be able to negotiate life as a householder." After some rehearsed hesitation, I relent and cancel my Kashi trip.

My wife announcing, "Lunch is ready," breaks the reverie. I stop digging up the past, satisfied I've junked enough of the past that didn't need to be remembered. Or preserved.

I Pulled the Chain

Platform No. 1 of Nampally railway station was known as Hyderabad B.G. under a different regime. The afternoon of a weekday, the western sun vengefully poured his molten lava on the waiting passengers and the friends and relatives who came to see them off and on those present to receive incoming passengers. In the crowd were my wife and I, headed for Chennai to meet the boy's parents. The other population inhabiting the platform included vagabonds wedded to minor crime, vendors of overpriced tea and biscuits, unleashed mongrels, and invisible CCTV cameras enjoying the troubled scene under their nose. A number of railway employees in white uniform of duty pompously measuring the distance between one end of the platform to the other added to the melee. A budding writer would see the scene as an unorganized reception committee waiting to welcome the incoming Secunderabad-Chennai Express.

Soon I began complaining of creeping heat and a feeling of giddiness. I touched my head to push back a flank of hair bothering my brow. It was all clammy and sticky. I cursed my Maker. Five minutes later, I felt unsteady on my legs, sensing a liquefication of my body. I looked for something to support my sagging body. There were no unoccupied plastic chairs on the platform. Luckily, the train rolled in onto the platform. We had two lower berths reserved. As soon as we entered the compartment, I spread myself on the berth.

"Are you okay?" my wife asked, her voice filled with anxiety. I didn't reply, signaling to her with my hand not to bother me. From experience, she knew all was not well with me. She touched my forehead and found it scorching. It was hot inside and outside the compartment. The overhead fan leaped to life for a nanosecond and died.

Reading the terror on her face, a passenger occupying a window seat near our berth intervened and advised her to cover my torso with a wet towel. We had no idea of what distance the train had covered in the meantime. My wife asked the window passenger to kindly find out whether there was a doctor on board. There was none, he said, and suggested they stop the train and ask the guard to send a message to the next station to get a doctor to see what needed to be done. None, however, volunteered to pull the chain, knowing it would involve a penalty. My wife told the helpful passenger she would take the responsibility for pulling the chain and paying the penalty.

The Good Samaritan lost no time in pulling the chain. Anticipating the train stopping any minute, every passenger in the compartment showed interest in the ongoing drama. Reluctantly, the train stopped one station ahead of Bhongir. The guard entered the compartment shortly after. My wife told him that I needed immediate medical attention.

"Amma, I will send a message to the next station," he said. He hurried to the stationmaster's cabin. Two or three passengers followed the guard into the cabin. One of them ran back to the compartment shouting, "The message has gone to Bhongir." Now there was a crowd in the coupe, expressing anxiety and looking at me and alternately at my wife, who was now unabashedly crying and bribing every God to save her husband.

Fifteen minutes later, the train trundled into Bhongir. It came to a halt, and our compartment came face-to-face with the doctor, an elderly person, standing on the platform.

He and an orderly, carrying his bag, entered the compartment. He held my wrist and raised his right eyebrow to indicate how serious the case was. "Amma, make him swallow these Crocin tablets. He should be okay in an hour," he said, patting my wife's head in condolatory affection. That show of fatherly concern by the doctor breached her tear ducts. "No need to panic, my dear," he said and squeezed my wife's shoulder and left. Seeing the doctor depart, the guard came in and asked me whether the train could resume its journey. I smiled at his courtesy.

My wife never stopped crying softly and pledging all the gold in the house and on her body to all gods and goddesses she had installed in our kitchen shrine. Shortly, the outside plunged into darkness. A stray light blinked, indicating the existence of a passing hamlet in the distance. Slowly I slipped into a deep torpor without a thought for my wife and the state of panic I had left her in. I knew my wife's emotional fragility because she had been my alter ego for more than three decades. She had never existed as a separate person. I was her raison d'être. In her daily prayers, she sought a long life for me and nothing for herself. When we had a daughter, she acquired an additional charge. Her attention to me and my daughter was such that people thought she had reduced herself to an unbeing.

Against the background of the train's rhythmic rattle, neither of us was in a state of consciousness familiar to the ordinary person. The surge of emotions was such that without being conscious in a human way, we abandoned the present as a setting for existence by traveling to a past and remembered how, with the birth of our daughter, we had ceased to exist emotionally as two entities. The baby's arrival had fused us into a joint being with two bodies but a common mind, receiving, storing, retrieving, and reacting to stimuli from our environment.

Over the years of our spousal life, we managed to build an invisible telepathic bridge. I knew she was peeping into the pages of our unwritten autobiography. Our wedding performed under a vast canopy of palm leaves attended by hundreds of uncles, aunts, cousins, friends, classmates, and the town's gentry, our joint craving for a baby girl, the delight of bringing her up, our health setbacks. The night our daughter was hospitalized and the doctors said chances of recovery were slim—and even if she survived, they were not sure of the damage the brain might have suffered—we had cried, with the eyes of patients and their relatives on us.

We had cried in moments of happiness too when she was the first student from her school to win the national talent scholarship. When she was about to board a flight to the US for a doctoral degree, we broke down in the airport lounge, telling her we would cancel the ticket if she didn't want to leave us. Now, we were on our way to meet the parents of the boy she wanted to marry... but this calamity.

In the train, I thought of none but myself. Would I be around when we reached Chennai? It did not enter my mind that in her hour of distress, my wife needed solace from me. Did she sleep? Did she have food? Nothing of the sort occurred to me.

In my mind my self assumed the dimensions of a Viswaroopam. Whenever I remember that terrible journey, I feel ashamed and small.

The train pulled into Madras Central, bringing the dawn in its wake. As if it were in answer to my wife's prayers, I woke up resurrected and less mortal. The feeling of funereal proximity that stayed with me throughout the journey disappeared. She shed tears in delight and gratitude to the multitudes of her gods.

But the man who was supposed to receive us at Chennai was nowhere to be seen on the platform. We had no idea what he looked like. Nor were we sure he would recognize us. We found a man in a white shirt over a white *veshti* standing before the weighing machine. He might be the man supposed to meet us, I thought. I approached him and said, "Sitaraman?"

"Yes," he said with a sigh of relief.

The end of a nightmare.

It's Good to Watch TV

It's not easy to get a builder to accommodate the request of a single flat owner to make changes in the interior structure of the flat. On the strength of our having already bought a flat in another complex, we got him to erect for us in the living room of the second flat we were buying a long glass shelf along its northern wall, rising three feet from the floor. Poor man, he caved, doing whatever we wanted him to. We kept this concession as a secret lest other buyers too pressure him to extend them the same favor. We high-fived our little victory. Didn't someone say life, after all, is a collection of small and big victories and defeats?

We filled the glass and masonry shelf with books we'd brought from Delhi as part of our intellectual pretensions. Some of the books were borrowed, forever. Some came to me for review. We, my wife and I, argued an entire day, bruising our vocal cords, about whether the books should be lined up in alphabetical order of their titles or according to the size of their spine. We did neither. We just let the books fall into a disorder of their choice. The marble top of the shelf became for us a long and low mantelpiece on which we showed off some nonliterary cargo: two toy horses made of leather by Rajasthani craftsmen and gifted to us by Thiagarajan, our neighbor. We didn't check with him about the breed, remembering the old advice about not looking into the mouth of a gift horse. Both are saddled and ready to ride. They have uniform coffee complexion. If God were human, as His devotees believe He is, He would invest these chargers with life and ride away. I would do the same thing if I were God.

On the marble tarmac, we parked a toy red Albion double-decker bus such as the ones we'd seen on the roads of Hyderabad on our first visit. The first elevated runway for any bus in the country. On top of a library. I look at it fondly, remembering how as children we would run up the spiral stairway at the entrance of the bus, sit on the upper deck, and look down on the tops of foreign cars and sun-scorched scalps of the pedestrians. Great fun it was to ride from Charminar to Ranigunj. Not anymore. Some urban arts dork took them off the roads. They later surfaced in Central Park, New York. A replica of a derailed steam locomotive I'd played with as a child also claimed space on the top of the marble counter, without its steam and steel mass. Tokens of middle-classness, you might say. We also kept a few porcelain figurines of European men and women my father had brought from Dresden for my sister long, long ago, beyond the reach of memory. My childless sister gave them to me to pass on to my daughter. At the wall end of the shelf sat our new BPL color television set in a diagonal position. When it is switched off, you can see the kitchen counter appear on its screen. It reflected the gas stove readily and, if you strained your eyes, the Corelle crockery my daughter brought from the US on her first visit.

Our builder, squat and stumpy, walked in one day and said the placement of the TV violated the laws of Hindu architecture, Vastu Sastra. We waited for him to leave and laughed behind his back.

We watched very little TV in the morning when the crush of daily chores ruled out such indulgence. When we bought our first black-and-white Crown TV in Delhi, we could get only

Doordarshan, the media-maligned state television outfit, for a couple of hours in the morning and four hours in the evening without advertisements. The transmission closed with Salma Sultan or Protima Puri reading out the Hindi news from a tele-prompter and ending the bulletin with a smile that needed some effort to eject. Teleprompter was a novelty at that time. We ac-quired a color TV when we shifted base to Hyderabad and con-tinued to consume Doordarshan's Spartan fare.

George Bush and the Gulf War came, through no fault of ours, a couple of years after our arrival in Hyderabad, after a long exile in Delhi. The TV showed images of the war and the skies lit up with color and Patriot missiles setting the desert skies on fire. It re-minded us of July 4 pyrotechnics in New York across the Hudson, close to where our daughter lived. Soon the number of channels multiplied, and we had to change to a BPL color set with a magic wand that changed channels as if it read your mind. That set, the gift of the Gulf War, is the protagonist of today's story. The moral of the story is embedded in its title. For a few months after we bought the new TV, we marveled at the magic of the remote to shuffle channels at our will. We could never enjoy the programs unless the remote was in our hands.

When we first saw a remote in *Ek Baar Phir* featuring Deepti Naval filmed in London, we were amazed at what technology could achieve. Taking over our minds. Though my wife and I were united in amazement, we couldn't stop the remote from becom-ing a menace to domestic peace like Siachen between Pakistan and India. Each would part with it to the other with an air of martyrdom and unconcealed disgust.

At the time of this story, there were at least fifty channels, and I would go on hopping from one channel to another till my wife snatched the remote from me and delivered a lecture on mature behavior. If you had the time, you could see at least a dozen movies in a day. Then there was this fashion channel for lovers of wardrobe malfunction. Models reveled in textile minimalism. Remember Janet Jackson? This channel choice aplenty called for mechanics of mutual agreement and understanding that, like Indo-Pak détente, we didn't have in ample supply. So, we were both happy and unhappy with the TV. Life is a mixed bag. We also agreed that however much we loved each other, TV and love were two different things.

The TV held us together for most part of the day in a state of conjugal tension, alternating between bickering and bonding. Short of writing it down, we came to an understanding that my role was to simply stand and stare when serials of my wife's choice were aired. This understanding marked our watching a film that evening when the defining event of the story began closing in on us stealthily like blood pressure. The movie was *The Burning Train* featuring a gaggle of heroes and heroines. Dharmendra and Hema Malini were my wife's favorites even after they had married and had children. My favorite Madhubala had died long ago.

"What kind of outfit is that Dharmendra wearing?" I comment unwarily, forgetting our understanding and raise my wife's hackles. Prickly girl.

"Why don't you watch the film? Commenting on everything as if you are very perfect," she shouts at me without taking her eyes off the awkwardly gallivanting Punjabi guy thumping the screen. It is the aging hero that made me open my mouth, my wife doesn't realize. With my right hand, I seal my mouth and turn toward her to show I've carried out her writ. She is amused and endows me with a wifely smile, making sure the romping hero is not watching us. The smile was not meant for him. Poor girl, my wife, she never gets angry with me except when she loses her feminist temper.

The gangly Amitabh Bachchan appears on the screen with his ungainly steps and a body that appears to have emerged from a medieval rack. "I can't stand this guy. He should stop acting," I mumble to myself. Much against my calculations, the mumble reaches, traveling on what vicious wind I don't know, the ears of my wife. I brace for another show of anger.

"My god, can't you sit quiet till the movie is over? Leave me alone for a while," she says, raising her voice. I evaporate.

Making sure there has been a change in conjugal weather, I come back when the scenes of the burning and speeding train are lighting up the living room. We are now friends again and watch together the blaze with interest and anxiety. The train is speeding into a dark nowhere with half of its cars ablaze. At that point, I see in the right corner of the BPL a set of flames that look like a chain of orange pyramidal mountains. They are distinct in a three-dimensional way from the indolent fires of the burning train. Then I find a part of the kitchen come alive over the TV screen. I sense imminent danger. "Come!" I frantically call to my wife and dart into the kitchen.

One of the two burners of the stove we had switched off before sitting before the TV is burning. In a fraction of a second, I detect that the fire spread without the assistance of wind or an accomplice to the stove's tube connecting it to the gas cylinder. With a terror-stricken face, my wife reaches for the water canister in the kitchen alcove and empties it on the blazing burner. Riding on the tube, the flames now reach kissing distance off the mouth of the cylinder. I really don't know how it occurred to me to turn off the valve of the cylinder. When I did that, the fire died down at once, as if responding to a command of the gods. Another second or two, my wife and I would have become smithereens and a memory.

We stumble back from the kitchen into the living room, each able to hear the drumming of the other's heart. The TV is still coping with the fires of the smoldering train. It has stopped at a station where fire tenders summoned go into instant action. The burning cars are detached from the train. The platform is full of water. Relatives of the passengers, gathered after learning of the fire, rush toward the cars. There is a lot of hugging in relief among the parents, children, and friends of the passengers and tears of joy. And a huge crowd of unconnected onlookers and TV crews pushing through the throng to interview survivors.

My mind is too clogged to imagine the sort of obit that would have appeared the next day if we hadn't escaped certain death. We needed some one's shoulder immediately. We call our friend Surendra and his wife, Sailaja, and ask them to come up at once from their flat a few floors below. They come up three flights, suspecting from the tremor in our voice that something out of the ordinary happened.

"What happened?" Surendra asks me.

I'm still dazed and incoherent in my speech. My wife sits on the sofa, not registering their arrival. She is crying. Sailaja posts herself next to my wife, gently patting her on the back to take the fright out of her. Surendra asks Sailaja to go down, make and get some tea. They coax us to drink tea. After tea, we become who we were before the mishap.

"What happened?" Surendra repeats his unanswered question.

"Don't ask me," I tell him, meaning it is too scary to be narrated.

My wife tells them the whole story in unconnected bits and pieces.

"You've done a foolish thing. You should have come down immediately and let the cylinder explode and do its damage. You've risked your lives. It's a miracle that both of you are alive and telling us the story," Surendra chides us.

The four of us go into the kitchen. Surendra inspects the innocent-looking wet tube. It shows no wear and tear. The floor was wet with the water my wife emptied. And some water fell on the food receptacles we'd kept ready on the kitchen counter for our dinner.

"We will buy a new stove," my wife tells the couple.

"Let's go now and buy it," says Surendra.

We go to one of the shops on Abid Road. Surendra examines several stoves before approving one. We come home and thank Surendra and Sailaja for reviving us.

It's now three hours after our brush with death. It would be eight thirty in the morning in the US where my daughter and family live. We call her and tell her the story. She yells at us both and repeats her advice for the tenth time to come away and stay with them. "You would have made me an orphan," she cries.

That night, we couldn't sleep well thinking about what would've happened to us if we had not been watching TV. We learned a lesson: always watch TV.

A CARGO OF KNIVES

You go to sleep in the afternoon, wake up late in the evening, and think it is morning. In the misty transition between dream and wakefulness, you dangle between belief and disbelief. My wife, who was a player in one such happening, is no more to unscramble my dilemma. The period was May 1990, and the locale was foreign. Now I will let you into the details of the fact/fiction: Our flight to India takes off at 8:00 p.m. My wife and I leave New Providence at 3:00 p.m. There was no Liberty International Airport at Newark at that time. We get on to 78 West. The long drive to JFK, the check-in, customs and immigration, and the wait at the boarding counter compel us to leave early. My son-in-law drops us at Air India terminal at JFK and leaves us to put the car in the parking lot. We enter a verandah not protected from the temperatures raised by the western sun.

Some airline's busybody materializes, suddenly asking the passengers to open their trunks and suitcases so tightly packed that once unpacked they cannot be repacked. I wonder whether this is a kind of roving check-in. We are still some distance away from the heart of the story because immigration remains to be gone through. The story raises its head when at customs a random check reveals a couple of kitchen knives in our carry bag. This happened a decade before the destruction of the WTC Twin

82

Towers and the US campaigns in Afghanistan and Iraq. We could not put the knives in check-in baggage because they—the bags, not the knives—had already traveled to the aircraft hold on the moving carousel.

"What do you want us to do now?" I ask the customs man.

"You should hand them over to the stewardess, who will hand them over to the ground staff at Mumbai. When the plane stops at Mumbai for you to collect boarding passes to Hyderabad, they will be delivered to you on production of this receipt," he says, writing down the receipt and giving it back to us. We collect the document and get into the fully occupied plane, eat the airlines' smelly food, and sleep without a nightmare. I didn't check whether my wife had any. With a halt in London, we fly over the seven seas and arrive at the Chatrapati Shivaji International Airport. After the aerobridge moves into place to align with the plane's boarding door, we troop out, pushing each other and trampling upon shod feet. We form a quick line to collect boarding passes for two for Hyderabad. That done, we go on checking with airport busybodies to find out where we might collect the knives. The twelfth busybody does us a great favor by telling us where to go. We go to the kiosk we were told to go to collect our things and stand before the counter, waiting to be addressed. Five minutes pass without the man looking at us. Then I shout at him in Queen's English. Like an obedient colonial poodle, he asks us, "Yes?"

I show him the receipt. "No, sir, we haven't received any knives," the kiosk man says.

"What do we do now?" I ask him.

"You may check with Air India cargo during working hours," he tells us. The next day, we call the cargo office several times. No response. We ask a cousin of ours whether he has friends in Air India. He has. We give him the receipt. Days pass without anything happening.

Perhaps we didn't bring any knives from the US. We thought we had, but we didn't!

BURGLARY AT D 18

My daughter and my wife were coming home from a trip to Guntur. They went there to attend the wedding of my niece. Their train, the Andhra Pradesh Express, would, if it were on time, steam into the New Delhi railway station at 1:00 p.m. My plan was to leave home at eleven, spend some time in my office, and from there proceed to the railway station at twelve thirty. I secured the front door of our terraced, second-floor flat with an Aligarh lock. I pressed the shackle into the body of the lock and pulled the body down to check whether it was properly locked. I bolted the other doors from inside. Next, I opened the door that led me out on to the stairway. I put an Aligarh lock on it and checked whether it was locked in securely. I climbed down past the two flats on the first floor and the owner's house on the ground floor.

I left Hauz Khas at eleven, hailing an auto. I reached my office in Link House opposite the University Grants Commission. Arts editor Goel was free. We talked about art, Krishen Khanna, Jatin Das, and Swaminathan. He said the art capital was Boston. I said it was New York. I had the tea Goel offered and checked my watch. It was time to go to the station.

In front of my office I got into a Delhi contraption mounted on a three-wheeled chassis. It was known as *phut phuti* and shuttled between Link House and the Statesman House on Barakhamba Road on the outer circle of Connaught Place. On its way, the noisy vehicle passed Tilak Bridge, Lady Irwin College, Sapru House, Mandi House, Sahitya Akademi, and Modern school before it stopped at the Soviet Information Centre a few feet short of the Statesman House. I paid one rupee to the *sardarji* and got off at Connaught Place. I walked down to State Road and entered the platform via the back fence.

The loudspeakers shouted in two languages through the rumble and roar of passengers and vendors of cigarettes, cool drinks, beverages, and books that the train was on time. In another five minutes, I saw the front of the WDM 2C diesel engine near the outer signal hauling the Andhra Pradesh Express, tired from its trek across several states. Soon the train was running close to the brow of the platform. I stood three feet away. The cars were whizzing past the platform, I, I A/C, II A/C, II Sleeper Car, II, General, and so on. The train seemed to plunge into the heart of Pahargunj.

In a blur, I caught a glimpse of my daughter waving at me. I waved back and sprinted to where their car was likely to stop. At the entrance of the sleeper car, I saw her in *salwar kameez* and behind her the face of my wife, tired from travel and motherly care. I helped them disembark with their bags. A coolie in red uniform snatched their bags. After haggling, he settled for ten rupees. The coolie brought the bags out to the median separating the station building from the taxi line. He demanded fifteen. He was ready to make a scene. We paid him fifteen rupees.

The taxis next. The first cabbie said hundred rupees. The second demanded ninety, three times more than what the meter would read. It was hot outside. To escape the sun, I agreed to pay sixty, and the cabbie said okay. After a half-hour run, the taxi stopped before our two-storied house in Hauz Khas. My wife and daughter pulled out the bags from the trunk and went up to the second-floor flat. Then a shouting match ensued on the road in front of the house. The cabbie said he had quoted ninety. I said it was sixty.

"Dad," my daughter cried from the terrace of the second floor.

"What?" I shouted back.

"The house has been burgled," she said. I had no time to argue with the cabbie. I paid him ninety and ran upstairs. The front lock was broken. The lock of the flat on the terrace was also broken. The neighbors gathered to see the damage.

Someone called the police. The policeman from the Hauz Khas police station began to comb the house to check whether things were missing. Some coins of smaller denomination were missing from the small shrine in the kitchen. Some music tapes had also been pilfered. My daughter found that the gas cylinder and its regulator had disappeared from the kitchen. The policeman wrote a report, read it out to me, took my signature, and left.

My wife and I were relieved to know that nothing valuable was taken. We laughed at the burglar's poor luck because there were no valuables in the house. What about making tea or cooking the night meal? When this question came up, I ran to the colony market and brought an electric stove. This was no substitute for a gas cylinder and regulator. I visited my gas agency. I explained what had happened to the man at the agency. The gasman said their business was to supply a cylinder if the customer had a permit from the Gas Authority of India. Next day, I dashed off to the

GAI office. An official there told me without even looking at me that there was a long waiting list and my turn may come after two years. With the help of a newspaper friend, I approached the big boss at GAI. "Let him apply first," he said.

A fortnight after the burglary, a policeman called to say that the burglar had been arrested. They recovered twenty cylinders from him. Another journalist friend took me to the police station and got the station officer around to deliver a cylinder on the condition that it would be produced as case property before the court whenever the case came up for hearing. My neighbor helped me bring it home. I also laid my hands on a used regulator, paying the owner seventy-five rupees. The home fires began burning again. My wife was happy.

Three months passed. A policeman climbed the two floors of my building. He pressed the bell. I answered. The policeman said it was a summons to appear before the court with the case property. The cylinder had to be carried down two floors. It had to be ferried to the Patiala House court. The court was on the second floor. If I didn't comply with the court, I would be charged with contempt of court.

I sought the help of my newspaper's legal correspondent. He spoke to a lawyer at the court. The lawyer said, "Let not your friend worry. I'll take care of it." On the date of the hearing, I met the lawyer. The lawyer spoke to the magistrate. I had to attend the court, but the judge did not insist on producing the case property. After several hearings, the public prosecutor told the court that the accused had jumped bail. The court adjourned the case indefinitely. But the cylinder at my house continued to be court property.

During the respite caused by the accused jumping bail, I retired from my job and moved to Hyderabad and out of the jurisdiction of the Delhi court. I have no clue about what happened to the case or the accused. Before leaving Delhi, I surrendered the cylinder to the gas agency and obtained an acknowledgment of delivery. On the strength of this acknowledgment, I obtained a new cylinder at Hyderabad. All's well that ends well.

THE SEASIDE BRIDE

It is rather strange that my parents are worrying each other over my marriage. For, in my country, parents see a daughter who has come of age and is yet unmarried as a burning brazier on their chest. A boy, on the other hand, is never too old. No matter, my mother nags me no end.

Tension has been building for some time between my mother and me. To escape her nagging, I come home late and leave early. But my mother has seen more years than I have known and can see through my games. One day, to explain myself, I go down to our renovated kitchen.

"Amma," I address her, clearing my throat. My voice sounds unfamiliar to me. I catch her facing the kitchen counter with the coffee paraphernalia spread on it like toys my kid brother would scatter all around him. Standing on a low stool, she fails to pay any attention to me. I gather a glimpse of her coffee-making expression from the shining stainless steel jar in front of her. Her face, distorted by the globular jar, has shed the smile that always dances on her lips. Did she swallow the smile in a moment of abstraction?

"Amma," I call her again with a trace of bravado.

"Don't talk to me," she says.

My face falls as soon as she delivers that sharp sentence of silence at me. She shoves the steel jar toward the sink like a striker in a carom game. Very unlike my mother, that show of temper. My mother, I conclude, is in no mood to open a conversation. I don't ask her for how long I should remain mute. I try to decipher what went wrong with her so early in the morning. My mind goes over recent events. I recall a rumor making the rounds at home that she had chosen a Bapatla girl to be my bride.

I calculate that I would not lose face if I persist in discussing the matter and fail. It is my mother, after all. So, I come to the point: "It is not that I have decided to remain a bachelor. Amma, I understand you are overworked. I'll find you a cook." I ready myself for a bit of tongue-lashing at this unseemly levity.

"Don't talk to me" is how the conversation between us opened. "You know how worried your father is," she continues now, her face still fixed on the spherical surface of the coffee jar, ready to empty its caffeine contents into six freshly washed china cups.

"What about?" I ask her, my mind now focused on the beverage.

"You ought to know," she says, not wasting her words.

"I really don't know," I tell her, feigning innocence.

"It's about your marriage," she says.

"What's so urgent about it?" I ask her in irritation unbecoming of a son raised by her. "It can wait," I mumble.

"Wait? How long?"

"Amma, there's no law for a maximum age for marriage. Anyway, give me some time," I tell her.

She says nothing. It means we're not on talking terms thereafter. Silence is her weapon, and it never fails.

My mind is full of figuring out ways to get the smile back on my mother's face and get her to talk to me again like old times. She is not used to suffering the presence of an unmarried person of marriageable age. She detests celibacy as if it were some kind of a cancer. Perhaps Amma is afraid I will die heirless. But where is the empire the heir would inherit? Anyway, what Amma wants me to do after all is see the girl and marry her if I like her. I'll tell Amma I will see the girl, and everything will be fine. On second thought, I find that line of thinking too rash. I don't say anything more to my mother that would amount to a clear promise.

"Does everyone born marry?" I want to ask, but knowing she hates such stupid questions, I stop myself.

Seeking a breather from Mother's sulking, I go out to look up a cousin of mine living by herself on the YMCA road. She is not married. But she is happy. I must tell my mother about this: how people remain unmarried and yet (and therefore) happy. I will listen to music at my cousin's place to calm my nerves. Maybe Hirabai Barodekar. Seeta lives in a studio accommodation opposite Reddy College for Women. It is on the second floor of a building reached by a spiral stairway that is as fragile as my cousin. The stair head provides a view of the quad of the women's college that sits enticingly on a large tract of grass. It is overrun by the gaiety and flamboyance of girls, free of today's care and dreaming of an unyoked tomorrow, some wearing salwar kameez and some *odhni* and lehenga. A galaxy of maidens whose youth is on the verge of shedding innocence and who yearn to hear the melody of wedding pipes. I suppress a bachelor's temptation to wave randomly to one of them. I catch a girl smiling at me. I smile back. Her smile disappears.

My cousin's studio resembles Maharaja Parikshit's refuge, resting on a single pillar in the middle of the sea. I tap on the studio's open front door and wait. My cousin keeps it open to steal the capricious November breeze. The rap on the door brings her out of the kitchen, which is dim like my mood at that time. She is wearing a white Tangail saree. Her saree has a train of embroidered black swans swimming at the border. There is no lake or water on the border though. She blows an innocent smile, displaying her tiny teeth, abode of as yet undetected future cancer. Her eyes become two chinks when she smiles. She is dusky, the color of the earth after rain. She motions me to a wicker stool imported from Delhi.

"Please sit. I'll join you in a minute. I'm making tea for both of us," she says, a preamble now familiar to me. Her words sound like they are climbing out of a deep well as she disappears into the dark nothingness of the sooty kitchen.

"Welcome," I shout back my endorsement of the tea idea.

My inconstant eyes scan the room and settle on its meager inventory. There is hardly any furniture in the room, barring a dresser with a mirror that has lost its silvering in many places. Looking into the mirror, one would believe parts of one's body were eaten into. On the dresser is a rummage: a Jessore comb, hairpins, a barrette, and a number of things women accumulate for likely use in an unforeseeable future. The cousin's music notebook stares from the mat rolled out on the floor, checks the progress of my peripatetic eyes. The rolled-out mat is an indication that Seeta is all set to practice music. I bend down and pick up the music notes to check for additions to her repertoire. I riffle through the pages and stop when a passport-size black-and-white photo floats down from inside the book. I lean forward and grab the picture before it makes landfall, like a catch in the first slip. I look at it with my glaucoma-free eyes.

The photo shows a girl in her late teens in a half saree that conceals a blouse with sleeves reaching her elbows. The face is about to launch a smile. But her teeth, the very essence of a smile, are not visible. Her eyes seem to do the job. It is a black-and-white photo that throws no hint of the color of the saree or blouse. Seeta, my cousin, brings chocolate tea, a unique Hyderabad blend, in a tray that rattles from fright of an impending crash in her hands. I stretch my body like a slug to reach for one of the two cups and take it in my hand.

"Guess who she is," she says, certain I will say I can't. Perhaps the girl's identity is stored away in the heart of a parrot living in a forest reachable only after you cross seven seas, as it happens in many Indian folktales.

She slurps tea from the saucer like many people in Hyderabad do.

"I don't know. I think she looks like Jamuna," I tell her, too lazy to guess.

"She is your wife," she says and succumbs to gasps of mirth.

"I'm not married," I tell her as if she doesn't know.

"This is the girl Uncle and Aunty want you to bring home," she says and puts down the cup. Things seem to get interesting now. Is she that Bapatla girl my mother had in mind?

"Let's come to the point. Tell me, when are you going?" my cousin asks me, the question pregnant with multiple assumptions.

"Where?" I ask her.

"To the girl's place," she says and collects her cup for more slurping.

"What will I do there?" I ask her, though I know.

"You'll see the girl," she says.

"What girl are you talking about?" I ask her with a straight face.

"The girl in the photo."

"What *varnam* (first item in a Carnatic music concert) are you now practicing?" I ask her, trying to change the topic and disguise my bursting interest in the girl.

"We've learned ten varnams so far from Nookie," she says.

"Who are we?" I ask her. Nookie was my sister.

"Your wife and I," she says and laughs again loudly.

More than her resemblance to Jamuna, I find varnams a greater reason for making the girl in the picture mine. I adore varnams, and I adore the girl who sings them.

"Where're you? Are you listening?" she asks me, noticing the flight of my mind.

Where am I? I'm already there looking into Jamuna's eyes. "Carry on. I'm listening," I tell Seeta.

"You won't take your eyes off her if you see her," she says.

"You mean my eyes can't see anything else other than her?" I ask her.

"I know what you want. A fair girl. Good-looking and intelligent. She's all that," she says and collects the empty cups. A fancy comes over me. I let her withdraw into the kitchen. Assured she isn't around, I open the music notes and take a fleeting peek at the photo and kiss it. I've a hunch that I met this girl in a previous birth or some long time ago in a dream.

I reach home, my mind full of the girl, scenes of the wedding and the auspicious strains of the pipes in the background. That night, she appears to me in a dream and sings the viriboni varnam. I join her, and we sing it together.

The excitement of finding a way out of the impasse with my mother, who had vowed not to talk to me, drives me to our kitchen where my mother is getting ready to make the family lunch.

"Okay, Amma, I'll go see the girl," I tell my mother. The smile returns to her face after a long layoff, like the sun emerging after a spell of rain. She is my mother again. Off I go to Bapatla on a Saturday to see the bright-eyed photo girl, that Bapatla girl as my mother refers to her.

I take an overnight train pulled by a steam locomotive that looked like an Emmett caricature, belching smoke and soot. The kind you see mounted on a cement platform in front of the Kacheguda railway station, smarting under the sun and soaking in rain. I get into a compartment full of decibel-happy families returning from or going to a wedding. I climb onto an upper berth reserved for me. It smells of calico and the sweat of a previous passenger. I spread myself on the berth and find its upholstery ravaged.

A few minutes later, the train heaves out of the station leaving behind a disorganized commotion and chaos to grip the platform. The marriage parties open their food containers before the train reaches Bhongir. They serve themselves food, homemade perhaps, on paper plates. They make a happy racket. The smell of food rises like steam to reach the upper berth and replaces the stink of a previous passenger's sweat.

From my vantage, I spy a young girl with the eyes of a doe and long hair decked in strung jasmines, imbuing the air with intoxicating fragrance. With a smile coruscating her bridal face, she asks me to join the food orgy. Perhaps her name is Annapoorna, the Goddess of Food and Nourishment. I release a smile intended to travel into her eyes, stay there, and thrill her being all the way to wherever she is going. "No," I whisper to her without taking my eyes off hers. I begin to consider her as an alternative. For a while, I wonder whether her people would ask me, on an impulse, to accept her hand if they knew I was a bachelor. I put Jamuna look-alike from the photo on hold for a while.

The train zips through the winter night, throwing a black shroud over the landscape on both sides of the track. Such is the hazard of traveling at night that you miss a lot of the coastal scenery, the lay of the land, the river Krishna and the marvelous rail bridge over it. I make up the loss by building in my mind a small house (in addition to a colony already housing my imaginary harem) by the sea where Annapoorna, who offered me food, and I will live when we get off the train. I doubt whether the small house I'm dreaming of building for the girl will ever take off. Poor Annapoorna; she is condemned to stay in my memory.

It is early morning when I reach Bapatla, hoping that the girl I'm going to see will look like the girl I met on the train. I don't see the girl who offered me food on the train or her people on the platform. Perhaps the party got off at some earlier station when I was asleep. I surrender the ticket stub to a man in white dozing at the gate on a high stool. Then I cut my way through sleeping bodies, immune to mosquito bites, sprawled near the ticket counters. I come out of the station. The weather outside is pleasant enough to tickle the birds on the ancient trees in the parking lot to sing Raga Saaveri. How do they know Saaveri is an early-morning raga? Maybe they roost next to my sister's place.

Bapatla is a middlebrow sleepy town like R. K. Narayan's Malgudi in many ways. It is where the Grand Trunk Express stops for a while, adding to the prestige of the town. It is within hearing distance of the nocturnal melodies of the sea in the Bay of Bengal. The locals breathe this knowledge as if it were the very oxygen of their life. It is a place well known for jasmines, eggplant, and briefless lawyers who outnumber litigants.

I walk down a short stretch from the station in the direction of the town, turn right, and when I reach the Bhava Narayana Swami temple, I turn left. The town's only main road takes off from the temple and ends where it is washed by the boisterous waves of the sea. Ten minutes later, I am standing before the Anjaneya Swami temple. It is closed because it is not time yet to open. From there, my bride-hunting sister's place is a stone's throw. She teaches music to the girl I'm going to see, the same girl in the photo hiding in my cousin's music notes, the same girl my mother refers to as the Bapatla girl.

I'm no stranger to Bapatla. On my way through the main road, I notice that the walls of several houses, eaten into by hungry sea breeze, remain untouched as if they were heritage structures. A first-time visitor is likely to think that the locals love to live on the town's main road lined by shops and restaurants on either side. All life in the town is compressed within a mile of a clock tower of uncertain age and make on the main road. People gather here in amorphous knots and discuss politics, economy, elopements, marriages, births, abortions, deaths, murders, films, matrimony, late running of trains, promotions, and raises in dearness allowance.

I reach my sister's two-storied house, built when architecture was in its infancy. Not far from there lives the father of the girl in the photo. An official of the posts and telegraphs department, he is a widower with a college-going son and three daughters in the care of three widowed grand-aunts. My sister teaches music to one of his three daughters, the Jamuna look-alike. My sister brings me coffee and, before it becomes lukewarm, pours out personal information about her disciple: her height and age; two inches shorter, twelve years younger and fairer than me. She topped the school-leaving ranks and was good at sports and elocution. With her father reluctant to send her to college in a faraway town, she is learning varnams from my sister.

The day after my arrival, on an evening my sister considers auspicious according to *panchangam* and blessed by sea breeze, Bava, my brother-in-law, and I get ready to go to the postal official's place to see the girl my mother has eyed for a daughter-in-law.

Telling us to wait, my sister sprints ahead of us for a few yards and turns back. She then tells us, "You can start now." She believes that when you set out on an important mission, a woman coming from the opposite direction is a good omen. After a nod from her, we take an unpaved road that passes the postal official's place.

After a few minutes, we are there. We pass through a small gate that breaks the run of a low brick and cement wall enclosing the front yard. In a corner near the wall is a jasmine creeper. We trek down a brief walkway and reach a veranda with a sloping roof. The veranda has two doorways for entry into the main house. An impudent crow sitting on the low wall wonders who we are. As we climb three steps to reach the level of the veranda, ducking a low beam, several chairs such as one is familiar with in government offices greet us. In two of them, we see two men in their late fifties. One of them, I surmise, is the bride's father. They look like they have been expecting us.

They see us and rise from their chairs and intone in unison like pages in a Sanskrit play, "Please come in." Both of them wear mustaches, short of bushy.

"Are we late?" asks Bava, part of tradition-sanctioned inanities people utter to start a conversation.

"Not at all," they say, because it is good manners to utter a lie. *Two amusing pretenses*, I tell myself.

We take our seats very close to the doorway that opens into the postal official's portion of the house. I look up, for no reason I can cite then or later, at the gabled roof of the veranda resting on palm rafters that make me wonder whether they are past their expiry date. Bava introduces the girl's father to me. His name is the same as mine. The father points to the person next to him and says he is his elder brother. The brother doesn't nod acknowledgment. He has a head that is bald or tonsured, has deep-set eyes, and is wearing a homespun, collarless white shirt buttoned up to the neck on a white dhoti. A red vermilion mark cuts across his forehead wreathed in wrinkles. He sits with his feet tucked under him. The other brother, younger of the two, looks much younger and muscular with a thick steel-gray mop. He has expressive eyes.

The brothers position themselves on the left side of the doorway that faces the road, to be able to talk to the womenfolk who are vaguely visible on the other side of the doorway. The younger brother, my namesake, asks me about the weather in Hyderabad. More irrelevance assails me before he looks inquiringly at his senior. The elder brother looks at his watch tightly wound around his wrist like a monitoring bracelet and indicates a go-ahead. The junior brother peeps into the yawning void behind the doorway and tells nobody in particular to usher in the girl.

Now the show begins. My wife in the making emerges unobtrusively from her passport photo and sits hugging her knees on a mat of palm reeds near the doorway separating us from the bridal gaggle in the background. Looking demure and abandoned, the varnam girl engages herself in determinedly appreciating the woof of the mat. She is draped in a sari of white chiffon with orange polka dots. An emerald necklace she is wearing is beaming off and on a spray of green tint on her placid face. She has a nose that resembles her father's, reddened by the embarrassment of playing the mannequin. Her oval face is framed by lustrous hair.

More of her features come into view as she gets up to join her sisters in the gray background. She smooths the ruffled pleats of her saree. Her hair is secured into a plaited braid that flows deeply down her back and dangles. Pinned into her hair is a string of jasmines and *kanakambarams*. The jasmines must have come from the creeper we saw at the entrance. Behind her hovers in the haze of winter dusk a huddle of women, presumably her grand-aunts, sisters, and neighbors. High above them is a bamboo trapeze suspended from the aging rafters. It serves as a clothesline. Below the clothesline are some bedrolls piled upon old trunks. The presence of the bride's retinue makes me uncomfortable. I wish for this charade to end at the earliest.

"Would you like to ask her any questions?" the bride's father asks me in a tone that suggests I should.

"It's okay," I say, not meaning to ask any. There's a sudden silence. It tells on the composure of the father and uncle, who move uneasily in their government chairs.

Trying to check the creeping vacuum, the elder brother asks, "How about some coffee?" Bava declines the offer, dismissing it as an afterthought. Now, there really is not much left to do except prolong the state of pointlessness. My eyes focus on two well-fed lizards on the wall, watching the proceedings, motionless. Abruptly, one of them swashes in a westerly direction to suck in an insect. The second one pretends to be dead.

Seeing my poorly concealed discomfort, the father rises from his chair, a signal suggesting that the session has ended. Bava and I stand up, preempting the revival of the charade. *This girl*, I tell myself, *is more comely than the girl that for a while stole my heart in the train the night before. She, the postal official's daughter, has a grace that reminds you of a Bapu drawing.* She looks at my back, thinking I am leaving. I look back, intending to take leave of the brothers. Without design, my eyes meet her smiling eyes. She blushes a deep red and lowers her head. Bava and I make appropriate leave-taking noises and walk back through a wall of silence to the small gate where we stop for a while, finding the father hesitant to ask a question. "I will send the girl's horoscope if you need it," he says.

"No, I have no faith in such things," I say. Politely.

"Okay, we will look you up tomorrow," he says, meaning he expects to know my decision in twenty-four hours. He and his brother watch us till we disappear at the bend of the road.

At Bava's home, my sister, her face swathed in a broad grin, greets us and asks, "What's the news?

"Okay," I tell her.

"I know," my sister says, delighted.

That very night, she relays my approval to the girl's side. They check the Hindu calendar and fix a date for the wedding. One suitor less for the train girl!

Believe Me, Please

Neither my uncle nor I have an inkling of what is coming in a few hours on this day. It is one in the morning. The city has gone to sleep after a tiring day. The vehicles are off the roads. A night bird shows its face for a moment and vanishes into the cavernous darkness. Another bird, unlike the one before it, appears and merges into the starless night whose hours are numbered. I have to take a train that leaves Bezwada at 2:00 a.m. Past midnight, I go out in the silence of the slowly decaying night to look for a rickshaw. Soon I find one near the Aurandalepet masjid. The driver is smoking a Ganesh beedi to keep sleep away. I tell him where to take me. The fellow demands more than what is normal because, he says, it is midnight. I agree and go back home in the vehicle. My luggage, a hold-all and a big trunk, is waiting on the porch to accompany me on the journey. The driver dumps the bags on the footboard of the rickshaw as if they are sacks of rice. There is no one at home to say goodbye to. My uncle, who could have waved goodbye, is coming with me to the station to see me off.

All set, I step out of the house. My uncle sneezes. "Bad omen," I mutter to myself. Calpurnia's portentous dream. We leave for the railway station through roads seemingly curfew bound until we hit the Grand Trunk Road. There are not many men or women on the GT when the night is on the verge of its daily death. Where we get on to Besant Road at Kowtha Center, we run into a river of drowsy filmgoers returning from night shows at Nageswara Rao Hall and Alankar Theater. Our rickshaw swims through the current and reaches the newly built arch bridge over the Eluru Canal. We wheel down the approach road that is paved only in my imagination. In five minutes, we, my uncle and I, are delivered onto the plaza in front of the biggest railway station we've ever seen. We pay off the rickshaw man without a hitch.

I engage a rickety porter in red uniform. On the breast of the uniform is a brass badge showing his number. Passengers hail him by his number. He is known as a licensed coolie. I help him lift the luggage on to his head. To cushion off the load, he wears a huge turban that looks like a big surgical bandage. He is walking ahead of us, looking straight into whatever comes into his tunnel view. We climb on to a footbridge that disgorges us on to Platform 2. My train is an east-west express that starts from Machilipatnam and reaches Marmugoa in the Portuguese territory the following day. Kind of a poor cousin of the Trans-Siberian Express. I need to change to another train at Hubli to reach my destination.

The platform looks like it is all set for a communal riot. In me it evokes images of Paul Theroux's *The Great Railway Bazaar*. With my uncle by my side, I wait on the platform for the train. To fill the time, I hum a Hindi film song of the forties. Shanta Apte, is the name familiar? The melody fails to reach my ears through the cacophony that is native to Indian railway platforms. A person balancing a stack of books in both hands coughs to catch my attention. He recites loudly the titles of the books for sale. Suddenly he depresses his voice and in a whisper utters close to my ear, left or right I don't remember, "*Kama Sutra*," and shows an illustration from the book to entice me. I ignore him, and he moves on to his next victim. I resume humming the Hindi song I had abandoned.

A small boy vending tea looks appealingly into my eyes that await an attack of glaucoma in a distant future. I ask him to make tea for two. I pull the porter aside and promise to pay two rupees more if he were to preemptively occupy a sleeper berth for me. I'm traveling Inter class. After a wait of five minutes, I sight the headlight of the speeding-in steam locomotive boring into the solidity of the night. I alert the porter. The meter-gauge train rattles in and screeches to a halt. There follows a bedlam we are familiar with and have anticipated: people running helter-skelter as if warned of a tsunami. The porter takes the hold-all and dives headfirst into the Inter car through a window without crossbars. He spreads the hold-all on an upper berth. According to railway etiquette, that has the force of legislation. The sleeper berth is now mine.

Next, the porter reaches for the heavy trunk. I help him lift it on to his bandaged head. Balancing it on his head, he enters the car and deposits it beneath the lower berth. I follow him into the car, check my berth, and dismiss him. My uncle, smoking a Scissors cigarette, posts himself near the window. He tells me to keep an eye on my baggage. I ask him not to worry. I sit down on the lower berth and release a sigh of relief for securing a sleeper berth. The idea of travel usually tires me a day ahead of the journey.

The train has begun to move reluctantly. My uncle keeps step with it and shouts into the car, "Send a telegram when you reach. Keep an eye on your baggage."

"Certainly," I shout back through the curtain of Scissors smoke. The train disappears from the platform as if David Copperfield vanished it. For me, the platform disappears.

I find a plaque embedded in the ceiling of the car in four languages, Telugu, Tamil, Marathi, and Kannada, languages spoken on the route covered by the Madras and Southern Maratha Railway. It asks passengers to beware of thieves on the train. Soon I fall asleep when, I guess, the train is crossing the engineering marvel that is the Krishna Bridge. A while later, I wake to a disorderly explosion of noises you associate with a platform about to receive a train. I feel the train at a standstill. I hear the sound of the locomotive hissing out steam and boys hawking tea, biscuits, cigarettes, and fruit on the platform.

I ask a passenger on the lower berth, "What station is this?"

"Guntur," he says and yawns ungainly. The yawn spreads the smell of freshly consumed meal.

"Please see whether my trunk is under the berth," I say to him, willing it to be there.

"I don't find any trunk here," he says indifferently.

Seized with panic, I get down and find the belly of the lower berth empty. Since the train doesn't stop anywhere before it reaches Guntur, I presume that someone walked out of the train with it soon after the train steamed into Guntur station. Everything, my money, my ticket, my clothes, is in that trunk. I'm left with the clothes on my body and some unwashed linen in the hold-all.

"Complain to the police," the passenger advises me. Word spreads to other parts of the car. Passengers tell each other stories of past thefts on trains.

"I'll do it at the next junction," I tell the man who advised me to report to the police. I remember a rule of the railways that if a person has lost his ticket, he should get off at the next junction and report it. How do I explain myself? Will the railway staff believe me? Suppose they let me off the hook. What do I do for food? Beg? How do I get back to Bezwada? Questions I have no answers for. My mind has become so numb that the loss has stopped bothering me.

The train reaches Dronachalam junction at around eight in the morning. A ticket inspector in white uniform posts himself in front of the Inter car, crouching like an animal sniffing for prey. I hardly get off the train when he asks me to show my ticket. I tell him it is a long story.

"Please stand aside," he tells me as he inspects tickets of other disembarking passengers. One by one, they show their tickets and head for the exit. The TI catches a man trying to elude him. "Show me your ticket," he demands.

The man is silent. The TI pushes him by the neck to a side and says, "Rascal, you want to throw dust in my eyes?" I stand behind the TI, wondering whether he will treat me in the same way. Will he hand me over to the police?

He lets the train pull out. He sees a policeman pass by and asks him to take the ticketless passenger into custody. He then turns to me. "What's your long story?" he asks in a voice neither polite nor impolite. I tell him the entire story. I also tell him I'm a law student on the way to Belgaum for my second semester. Normally, railway personnel dismiss such stories as bullshit. I don't expect him to believe me.

"Please follow me," he says. This "please" puts some cheer into me. I follow him, lugging my hold-all. He enters the railway restaurant. It is crowded. We sit at a table strewn with the crumbs left by previous users. The inspector shouts for a cleaner. A boy of ten comes running and wipes the tabletop with a mop dripping what looks like dishwater.

"What will you have?" the man in white asks me. This cordiality surprises me.

"I leave it to you," I tell him. He beckons the waiter and tells him to bring two plates of idli and two half cups of coffee. Not a word passes between us at the table.

The TI sits playing with his puncher. The food arrives, and I pounce on it, my teeth unbrushed. Breakfast over, the ticket man pays the bill.

"Let's go to the police station," he says.

"Why police station?" I ask him with a brave face.

"You'll register your complaint," he says.

We go to the police station, where I repeat my story. The policeman, sitting under a large picture of King George VI, betrays no indication of trust or distrust. He records my complaint. "We will look into it," he says with a face devoid of any expression.

The ticket collector and I, then walk down to the waiting room. I begin to feel like a character in a mystery novel. He asks me to rest, promising to call me again. For what?

As soon as the ticket man turns his back, I nod off without a thought for the future. What is there to think about?

At twelve thirty, my savior reappears. "Come, let's have lunch," he says.

My numbness now turns into daze. "Kind of you," I tell him. The railway lunch is always delicious when there is no train on the platform.

After lunch, he flourishes a pack of cigarettes in front of me. He asks, "Do you smoke?"

"No, thanks," I tell him. I go with him with a nonchalance that suggests I have a right to his hospitality.

"Okay, please rest in the waiting room. I'll wake you up at three thirty. There is a train that takes you to Bezwada."

I thank him again, embarrassed by his friendly manner. And I sleep again.

A policeman enters the waiting room after an hour. He taps on my shoulder and says, "Sir. The train will arrive in a few minutes. Wash up and get ready to leave." He doesn't mention who'll buy the ticket. I don't ask him either. I stop thinking about the next step, leaving everything to chance. In a short while, the Bezwada-bound train steams in.

"Please follow me," the policeman says. We enter a third-class car. The policeman finds a place for me. I sit. The policeman sits next to me. He makes no effort to leave the train and go back to the station. He tells me he will see me off at Bezwada. Four hours later, the train clangs to a halt at Bezwada. The policeman gets down, takes me to the exit gate, and tells the ticket collector at the gate that I am sort of a state guest. We are out of the station now. The policeman gives me a smart salute and takes leave of me.

"Thank you very much for everything," I tell him and stand there at the parking lot till the sea of passengers sucks him in.

I head home carrying the burden of disbelief. I'm not sure whether my uncle will believe my story or dismiss it as spin.

THE GIRL NEXT DOOR

At the heart of this story are a dream of gossamer texture and an ingénue who appears at the very end of the dream and walks away into the ambiguous line between dream and reality.

In a reconstruction of the dream in my waking hours, the girl and I happen to be in a French garden at the front of my grand-father's large house. I see the girl converse with the flowers in the garden. She pauses impulsively and kisses a flower and passes the moisture of her virgin lips to it. I approach her with a smile on my face and tell her with the confidence of an owner, "You can take home some if you love them."

"No, please, I can't hurt them. I am not a goddess to whom you can offer the flowers. Thanks, anyway," she says, charmed by the garden. "How lovely would it be if there were a swing here in the midst of these beauties and I could drive away all anxieties?"

"Come, that's no big task," I tell her and ask one of the men work-ing in the garden to fix a swing to a strong limb of the margosa tree at the entrance of our ancestral house. The worker, admiring the girl's love of flowers, makes the swing from freshly plucked marigolds, chrysanthemums, jasmines, and roses. I then ask her to sit on it. She sits tentatively, tightly gripping the flower-decked ropes on both sides of the swing. It is time now, I think, to give the swing four or five pushes from behind. That I do.

A peacock from the neighborhood nursery lands before the swing and unfurls its gorgeous tail of a thousand eyes, blue, green, yellow, and brown. Maybe the peacock came from Manmatha, the god of aesthetics, bearing a message for me or her or both. Indian mythology is full of tales of birds carrying messages between lovers. Unseen in the leafage of the margosa tree, a thrush breaks into a morning melody. The girl on the floral swing, the cocky peacock, and the chant of the thrush are straight out of a scene from an ethereal world of fantasy.

The girl loses no time propelling herself to a constant rhythm and thrill. When the swing arcs ahead, her Kanchi *paavda* billows like a parasol unfurled in rain. When it recedes, the green silk skirt sinks into the fork of her legs. The swing zooms higher and higher till it becomes horizontal at the peak of its trajectory. I see her face shine with excitement mixed with fright. The margosa casts recurrent geometry of light and shade on her slender, pendulating body. I now watch the slow and reluctant gravitational descent of the dry leaves of the great margosa mantle her head and raiment. After some time, she climbs down the swing of flowers. At touchdown, she totters and sways into my arms, standing near the swing. To avert a fall, she involuntarily hugs me and presses her flushed face into my chest. She stays unmoving in my arms until the wild throb of her heart levels off with my cardiac symphony. I take in her dark, sparkling eyes and enticing smile that seem to pull the beholder into her orbit. I look into her glowing eyes and ask, "Did you enjoy the ride?"

She half-closes her eyes and blushes a deep red. "Of course, I did. The experience is so new to me I cannot describe it. Maybe

I will tell you more when I have more of it," she says, then bites her tongue and looks away, embarrassed at her lack of restraint.

"What's your favorite flower?" I ask her.

"God has not created it yet."

"What is it that God has not created?"

"A chrysanthemum with the scent of a rose."

"Let us try to graft both of them in our garden."

"That would make my wish come true," she says and realizes she is still in my arms. She blushes and, smoothing her clothes, says, "I must go now," and softly pushes my arms from her waist.

"It's too early to leave. Do you have a garden at home?" I ask.

"Yes. Indeed, two. A small one in front of our house. We have chrysanthemums, roses, zinnias, and Decembers. But we have a large garden in the backyard, mainly for vegetables and fruit. We have two jasmine creepers too."

The dream dissolves when my mother calls me from out of nothingness, "Get up. Here is your tea." I come out of the dream with the scent of the girl's body and the satin touch of her half saree still hugging my consciousness. But the queen of the dream, her heartbeat, the swing of flowers, and song of birds, the diaphanous half saree have all vanished. Where could they've gone and how? A sense of deep loss and betrayal that follow the loss of an empire, and with it the empress, envelops my being. Was the dream unreal? Don't some dreams foretell what's coming?

I am sure that this dream will cease to be a dream soon. In the years that follow, nothing of the dream inhabits me except the smile and the eyes of the tormentor. With the help of the memory of the dream intact, I hope I will someday find the owner of those eyes and the smile. When I find her, I'll own her; her eyes and her smile will then be mine and mine alone. *Forever*, I tell myself.

Meanwhile, time doesn't stop ticking; days become weeks, weeks become months, and months become years. Years after that dream, we move to Hyderabad, following my father's impulsive decision to migrate. On arrival, we stay with an uncle who lives in Barkatpura, a few minutes' walk from the railway station. It is a prosperous district of the city. A short distance from my uncle's place is a lush, green, circular park popularly known as Barkatpura Chaman. Central to our story is this *chaman*, and occupying a large part of its periphery, a two-storied building where this story plays itself out. Its beauty glows in the simplicity of its design, a complex of four flats washed with white marble dust and a notion of milk. The moon lingers over the building longer than it does elsewhere, an old man soaking in the sun at the chaman tells us. My father traces the owner and rents two flats of the house. The owner has named it Anand Bhavan. The abode of bliss. No one passing by the Barkatpura Chaman ever fails to notice its understated majesty.

The chaman is both a traffic island and a park. With a few characterless cement benches like unfinished Henry Moore sculptures, and an ornate bracket of five domed lamps atop a wrought iron post in its middle, the park, like the *chandrakanta* flowers, acquires life in the evening, a time mothers and nannies bring children out to play and frolic. When they leave, the city's love birds arrive to exchange intimacies. At the beginning of the arc of the chaman is a cottage that looks like a hermitage of humble descent, separated from the aforementioned two-storied main structure by a low wall hiding behind a finely manicured hedge of hawthorn.

The time of this story is our tenth year in that elegant house, ten years after I left behind the dream I had in Bezwada. Thanks to my father's fatherliness, I stay at home after graduating in law. Besides looking for work, I do nothing more worthwhile than reading books and listening to music, something my father finds hard to object to. My idea of taking a break from books and music is to drag a low rosewood chair close to the large bay window of our living room. It catches a view of the chaman, where it is eternal spring, of the road ringing it, and of the passing show in the park.

One day, I park myself at our living room window for a casual survey of the world around the chaman. Involuntarily, my eyes begin a leftward movement to the finance secretary's mansion, where a gardener has just finished his job of watering the front lawns. He does it, rain or no rain. Then the eyes travel to Nawab Gulshan Yar Jung Bahadur's ranch house across the road that takes you to Osmania University; next my eyes take in the chief minister's residence under siege night and day by a milling crowd of petitioners, touts, and political brokers, some pitching tents on the footpath across his house, ready to swoop at sight on the chief minister's minions to wangle an appointment. Past the house of a friend of my brother, my eyes are about to complete the circuit when they refuse to get past the little cottage, arrested by the appearance of a nymph who dazzles like a streak of lightning. Or is it a fragment of the moon that appeared on earth as a result of a divine curse? Something tells me I've seen her somewhere. My God, could this nymph be the girl of my dream? The same eyes and the same angelic smile. Is this a continuation of that dream? The first thing I do after confirming that she is the dream maiden is to thank God for posting a friend in that humble dwelling. Could the margosa tree be the same one in front of my grandfather's house, transplanted magically?

It is December, and the dry yellow-gold leaves of the margosa float down gaily to carpet the compact unpaved courtyard of the cottage. My eyes wander to where my dream girl is raking the grounded leaves with a short broom, like Devika Rani in *Achoot Kanya*. The two children of the house trail her like kittens trailing a cat, picking up leaves with their tiny hands and gamely adding them to the pile. Between them, they make gathering leaves more a game than a chore. She glides about the place with balletic grace. She senses, I think, my eyes upon her and raises her head and traces their origin to my presence at the window. Our eyes meet, and each of us feels found out. At once, I appropriate her in my mind. A sense of ownership descends on me. She straightens up and lets the broom drop down to the ground and considers my eyes upon her. On her lips glistening with moisture spreads a sunny smile. Is it a smile of recognition? A smile that is worthy of celebrating in a sonnet. The girl comes across as proud and one who wouldn't shower her smile on all and sundry. When she bestows it on the beholder, she does it in style as if she is doing a favor. Does she recognize me as the one who helped her with the swing in my grandfather's garden of marigolds, chrysanthemums, jasmines, and roses? For a while, I imagine that everyone in that doll's house has left it to make room for her and me to live there, undisturbed. I've no idea whether my longing for her is love or some sort of infatuation.

Next day, I take my friend Joshi to the Irani café attached to Deepak Mahal Theater and extract some biographical detail about her. He tells me that she is from a village and has come to stay with her uncle, a middle-level official in the Revenue Department, to finish the last year of high school. Her father lives on his farm in their village near Raichur. She will be attending college next year.

With plenty of foresight, I dangle candy before the kids, years away from the ways of the world. Who knows when I might need their help? I've only six months to win her over. I will then leave home to attend advanced law classes. This signals to me the need to act fast.

The stars are on my side. One day, from my window vantage, I spy her heading for our house, leaving her entourage behind. At the behest of her aunt, I guess, she is coming to borrow sugar or coffee powder from my mother. Earlier, the kids used to come on such missions. She avoids the front door and floats to the back entrance opening into the kitchen. That's my mother's habitat. From the living room, I drift into the kitchen and surprise her. She raises her head and recognizes me as the man at the window. Did she see the same dream I saw at my ancestral home? A slow, reluctant smile rolls out leisurely across her lips, parting a crack to reveal a well-set string of teeth. We are now face-to-face for the first time. On a finely sculpted nose, she sports a red coral stud. She wears a mauve sari and a white blouse. Her smile never seems to desert her. I return her smile and ask her in Kannada for her name. She is surprised to hear Kannada in a Telugu household. Delighted, she smiles.

"What's your name?" I ask her to break the ice.

"I don't know." She smiles.

"I'll call you Anamika (nameless one) then," I tell her, looking into her eyes.

"If that pleases you," she says and takes her snaky braid into her hands and regards it fondly.

I look at the tresses and tell her what a pretty braid she has. A tinge of pink washes her cheeks.

"Why are there no flowers in your hair?" I say to keep the conversation going.

"Flowers are for gods and goddesses," she says with a glint of mischief in her eyes.

"Okay, tell me what flowers you will choose for your god," I say to her.

"I won't tell you now," she teases. She sees the cloud on my face and at once sets out to clear it. "Chrysanthemums with the scent of roses," she says.

My face brightens. Something tells me she is the same girl who appeared in the dream I had on the eve of our migration to Hyderabad. "Don't you remember me?" I ask her.

"You? How?"

"The garden, the swing, the peacock?"

"I'm sorry. But surely I would love to have been that girl in your dream," she says.

My mother is furtively watching us. She, my mother, smiles and playfully suggests I disappear. "Go mind your business," she says, waving me off, raising a ladle in feigned reproach. Seeming to enjoy my discomfiture, the girl smiles at me, as if I'd deserved the motherly snub.

"What do you want, my dear?" my mother asks the girl.

"My aunt wants a cup of sugar," she says in broken Telugu to my mother. My mother is taken in by her pleasing ways and, I presume, her eyes too. She gives her sugar in a small stainless steel bowl.

"Enough?"

"Will do. Thank you," she says without raising her head.

"I haven't seen you earlier …"

"I came only three days ago."

"On a visit?" my mother asks.

"No, I'm studying high school here," she tells my mother with restrained pride.

"Okay. Continue to visit us," my mother says.

"Visit us," I mimic my mother's words and voice.

"You haven't told me your name," says my mother.

"Vandana."

"Lovely girl," my mother says to me after the lovely girl has gone. The girl has to pass our front door to go back to the cottage. I appear at the front door as if predestined. I wave to her cheerfully as she walks back to her house. From the corner of her left eye, she watches me wave. She smiles and increases the pace of retreat.

Two days later, she is at the back door to return the sugar. My mother knows I will materialize there. She pretends to be busy and unaware of the girl's presence. In my mind, I thank my mother for her understanding. The girl sees me advance toward her and tries to spruce herself up. She yanks back a renegade *pallu* around her shoulder.

"What's the matter?" I ask her. She doesn't answer, implying she will talk only to my mother. She holds up the bowl full of sugar to me, smiling and avoiding my smiling eyes. I take the bowl from her hands and pass a note to her. I'm all keyed up. She might shred the note. Thank God, she accepts it, flashing an understanding smile that is a virtual reply to my note.

I continue to write notes; she continues to accept them but does nothing about them.

One day, I see her leaving home for her school, Sarada Kanyashala, in Sultan Bazaar. I wait for a few minutes, take out my Sunbeam bicycle, and catch up with her on the Kacheguda Station Road. I get off the bike and walk the bike beside her. "You didn't reply whether it's okay to meet at Yuvati Mandali," I say to her.

"I'm scared somebody will notice us," she says.

"We can meet in the park next to your school."

"Don't be in a hurry. Every moment has its ordained time," she says like a fatalist.

"Okay, there is nothing else I can do," I say, sounding hurt, and turn back.

At eight thirty, I turn off the radio after listening to Krishna Udayawarkar's Bhoop khayal. I move into the living room and pull the rosewood chair closer to the window that gives me a view of the chaman. School and university buses zip past before my eyes fleetingly. I sense some movement at the front door. The sylph and the younger boy are waiting there, expecting to be seen and hailed. The sylph and I exchange glances, revealing joy at seeing each other. Vandana is waiting, I presume, to see my mother to appear at the door connecting the dining hall to the living room. I turn my attention to the boy sucking his thumb. He is a cute brat with brown, curly locks and eyes full of mischief.

"Hi, Putta. Want me to take your picture?" I ask, opening the door. He doesn't say anything but looks at me to indicate it is okay. I go into the radio room and get my father's Voigtlander camera and drag a low stool into the middle of the living room where the light is best. "Put the boy on the stool," I tell Vandana. She lifts him onto the stool and sits him to face the window. He keeps his hands in his lap and restlessly anticipates the click of the camera. "Please hold him," I tell her.

I peer into the ground glass viewfinder and find enough light illuminating the boy's chubby face. I wait till he summons the right expression and click to take three frames. "Now your turn," I tell the sylph and look into her eyes for a sign of consent. She looks down at the carpet shyly, not saying a word. "Come, come," I try to persuade her.

Silence. "For my sake, please," I tell her.

She relents. "But these are yesterday's clothes," she says.

"Doesn't make a difference," I assure her and advance toward her to usher her to the stool. Before I reach her, she hurries and sits on the stool. She then gathers her long skirt in place. She is wearing a light green blouse with deep green checks on it and a skirt made of the same material. I'm now standing in front of her with the camera in my hand. A strand of her hair frees itself from her hairdo and dances in the air. I bend forward and caress it back into place. She grimaces but blushes nevertheless.

"Now look at me," I tell her. She is shy and smiles. Have I become a stranger suddenly?

"Okay, look into the camera." She becomes self-conscious and a bit tense. Now I employ an old trick of mine: get everything ready—frame, focus, light, and aperture—tell a joke, and click. This trick has never failed me. "Come, ready, don't laugh," I tell her. That makes her laugh. I lose no time and click, catching her at the penultimate moment of her restrained laugh. "Thank you, Vandana," I tell her.

There is relief and joy on her face. She rises from the stool and directs her glowing gaze at me to say thank you. The boy and she disappear into the dining hall to see my mother, their original mission.

Three days later, the photos arrive from the studio. When she comes out into her little garden, I flourish the pictures from my window, expecting her to come and pick them up. No, she sends the boy to me. But I give him only his photos and keep hers with me.

It is a Sunday, a holiday for the girl. As usual, I drift toward the window. She is there in the small garden among zinnias, periwinkles, moonbeams, and the jasmine creeper, watering them with affection. She stops suddenly and raises her head, perhaps to tease the koel hiding amid the margosa leaves. She trills, "*Koo, koo*," to the koel to provoke the bird. The bird picks up the refrain, and together they launch a duet. The duet has not progressed far when a spoilsport crow tries to crash into the concert. The koel flies away in protest. For the poor girl, it is the end of the musical engagement with the bird.

Next day, Vandana appears under the gulmohur tree overlooking my mother's kitchen, enjoying the soft rain of the tree's speckled red-orange flowers. She seems to have forgotten that she has come to borrow coffee powder or sugar. I appear there as if drawn by her expectation. "So, here comes the koel," I tease her.

She smiles beautifully, setting off a wave of exhilaration through my veins. "You know what the koel was singing?"

"How do I know?" she asks, a little irritated.

"It is Raga Hindol," I tell her.

She pretends she hasn't heard me. "Now let me go in. I want some coffee powder," she says.

"Okay, madam," I say in a theatrical way and let her step in.

"Come, my child," my mother greets her from the kitchen. "So, what do you want?" she asks the sylph with affection.

"Coffee powder."

"Do they teach music at your school?" my mother asks while filling a bowl with coffee powder.

"No."

"But my son loves music," she tells her.

Oh, Mother, I love you, I think.

That day, her uncle's family went out to see a film, leaving her alone at home. This piece of intelligence came my way from the kids in return for a couple of chocolates. I wait for dusk to dawn. There is no light in the porch of the cottage. The margosa tree checks the landfall of the moon, who is so bright that the front yard looks like it is paved with a carpet of snow. Under the trellised shade of the great tree, I move like a soldier wearing a white-and-gray camouflage and reach the front door of the cottage. Knowing well that he is not at home, I gently tap the door and call my friend by his name. She comes out and asks, in sign language, "What do you want?"

My nerves are a mess. "Is Ramu home?" I stammer.

"No," she says and suppresses a smile, lest it should imply an invitation.

"But he said I could come and collect the cricket ball we bought at Juneja."

"I've no idea. Come in. Look for it," she says, and steps aside to let me in, unaware of what is on my mind.

I enter the room and gently close the door behind me. I stand with my back to the closed door. I don't say anything. I gaze into her eyes and see in them my own dreamy eyes. She looks back into mine. Realizing how close she is to me, she steps back and moves away from me to lean against the wall. She is now staring down at her feet, perhaps counting her toes. More likely she is considering ways to negotiate an unfamiliar situation. She is confused like a character who has forgotten her lines.

I close the distance between her and me. I put my hands to the wall over her shoulders, weaving my hands into a ring. She is cornered in a pleasant way. We are now physically so close that each can hear the other breathe. It is a duet of the hearts. I ask her to sit by my side on an ancient trunk painted green. She doesn't move. I stand up, take her hand, and make her sit next to me on the trunk. I hold her soft hands; I can see the waves of ecstasy sweeping her as if they are tangible. The new hour of intimacy finds us trembling.

"Now, tell me what's on your mind?" I ask.

"Do you really need an answer?" she asks, twirling her scarf around her finger.

"I want you to be mine. May l ask you something?" I ask her.

"You've already asked," she says and looks shyly into my inebriated eyes. A feeling of impunity from the world descends on us. "What is it?" she whispers.

"Whatever it is."

"I assure you I'm yours. You may talk to my uncle," she says. These words touch the most mellifluous chord in my heart.

An impulse unsettles my composure. I let my left arm slide around her waist, and with the right, I raise her chin and softly kiss her tremulous lips. She shudders. The tremors find a rebound in me. She involuntarily weaves her arms around me. We share the ecstasy of first touch. She smooths her saree as if to expunge an indiscretion. Her eyes are a quaint blend of bliss and fright.

"Okay, thank you," I tell her and kiss her sparkling eyes and reach for the door. I walk out in a daze like Danny Kaye after kissing Virginia Mayo in *A Song Is Born*.

Amma is in the kitchen. Alone. I buzz around, fiddling with the freshly washed cups on the drain board of the sink. "What are you doing here?" she asks me without taking her eyes off the boiling milk on the stove. I grin. She knows why I'm moping around.

"Amma, will you do this for me?" She knows what it is because she has observed my state of abstraction and knows I cannot keep it to myself. "You know Vandana?"

"Yes, what about her?"

"I want to marry her, Amma." I don't know in what syntactical order the words tumbled out. Amma is capable of parsing them in whatever order they come out.

"Let me think about it," she says, taking the milk off the stove.

"What is there to think about?" I ask her, trying to place a lid on the milk.

"Everything," she says.

"Like what?"

"Don't be impatient like a school kid," she chides me. She notices the pain on my face and tells me she will talk it over with my father. "Let us see. I'll talk to Vandana's aunt and see how it turns out. You know her parents are poor."

"I'm not marrying her parents," I tell her.

It makes her laugh. She says, "We know nothing about them. No doubt the girl is good-looking and well behaved. Let's talk it out."

My mother is so gentle and amiable that I sometimes feel she has refined gentleness into a weapon. She has never raised her voice at her children or said a disagreeable word. I would rather readily hurt myself than hurt her, I resolve, and smile at her to show her son is unhurt. I go over my predicament and decide to accept what destiny has in store. I draw strength from my mother. She is there to absorb any disappointment.

Amma calls Vandana into the kitchen one day. She steps into my mother's parlor with trepidation. Amma understands her nervousness. "I want both of you to be happy. Tell me without fear, what is happening between you?"

"Nothing, Aunty," she says.

"Do you like Krishna?"

She nods affirmatively and makes an attempt to check tears.

"Why do you cry, my child?"

This word of affection tests her restraint, and she sobs into the *pallu* of her saree.

"Do you think your parents will agree?"

"I'm not sure," she says.

"I will talk to your aunt. Don't lose heart," my mother tells her. Vandana continues to cry. My mother hugs her to calm her. She recovers after a few minutes.

"I'm grateful to you, Aunty," she says, sobbing, and leaves.

It is already a week since Vandana has appeared under the great margosa tree or in my mother's domain. My left eye is twitching. I worry that's not a good omen. Where has she gone? The kids are of no help.

"Uncle, she has gone home," they tell me.

"Where?"

"How're we to know?"

Joshi confirms this story. He can't tell why she disappeared abruptly. My mother volunteers to probe. She meets the girl's aunt. "Did you get any word from her parents?" my mother asks her.

"Yes, we did," says her aunt, averting her eyes.

"What did they say?"

"I'm sorry. They don't favor the match."

"Strange. But why?"

"It's an unequal relationship, they think. They can't match you in any respect. They are scared," she says.

On her return, one look at my mother's face tells me everything. "Okay, Amma. Don't brood over it," I tell her.

It is a denouement that shakes me. I go back to Somerset Maugham and A. J. Cronin to escape the torrent of memories. My innate hatred of self-pity and melodrama save me from total disintegration.

My dream girl is never seen again.

PICNIC

When this incident happened, I was nine years old. It was a Sunday evening in winter as I returned home from a private class called by my science teacher. The sun was in a hurry to disappear into the west, and it was neither cold nor warm. The big house my grandfather had built was unusually silent, as if the occupants had evacuated it, fearing the river Krishna would impulsively rise and drown the city.

I went up to my room in the penthouse where my parents and siblings lived. None of them were there; instead, I found the night watchman making our beds for the night.

"Where have they all gone?" I asked him.

"For a picnic at the farmhouse," he said.

A feeling of rage at that act of betrayal swept through me. *They need to feel the hurt I have suffered,* I thought. The farmhouse was built adjoining the Grand Trunk Road passing north of our house. The road was a straight stretch for a long distance like the runway of an airfield.

My anger was extended to the poor watchman too. I left the house without telling him. He would have to explain my absence to my uncles when they came back from the picnic. It was dark as I stepped out; the only illumination came from the municipal street lighting of halogen bulbs. They could hardly pierce the dense gloom of the winter. The roads were empty of pedestrian or vehicular traffic, like they would be under a curfew. Walking on the roads at that time was like a walk through a large cemetery reeking of death.

Crickets and idle insects of nature that come to life after dark began playing an elegiac orchestra. I walked through this desolation and eeriness like a man possessed and reached the end of the town landmarked by the Muslim burial ground. The street lighting too stopped there.

From there, the great Grand Trunk Road of debatable antiquity entered a tunnel walled by dense tamarind trees on both sides of the road. My destination was three miles through this tunnel. The darkness and the silence of the Grand Trunk tunnel resembled the cosmic vacuum that greeted the birth of the universe. But a full moon shone through the leafy walls of the tunnel. I forged ahead, propelled by a primeval anger such as Shiva releases through his fiery third eye before he launches upon his Tandava dance of destruction.

On the way, walking ahead of me, a turbaned local alerted by my footfalls behind him stopped and waited for me to catch up with him. When I did, he asked me, "Boy where are you going in this darkness at this time?"

"I hate them. How mean of them to leave me alone at home and go on a picnic."

"Who are they?"

"Do you think they can escape me?"

"You didn't tell me who they are. My dear boy, I will take you wherever the picnic is."

"Promise?"

"Promise," he assured.

"It is our farmhouse at Gunadala," I said.

"Okay, I am going beyond Gunadala. I will drop you at the farmhouse and tell them not to punish you for this adventure. Okay?"

The local and I covered more than a mile when it occurred to the man that I could be hungry. "Are you hungry?" he asked me.

"I am," I told him.

He opened his palm and with his index finger wrote "banana" on it. Instantly a banana materialized in his palm. I took it and ate it avidly, even as my system refused to accept what it had witnessed.

"Are you surprised?" he asked me.

"No, I'm stunned."

"You want to know the secret?"

"Who wouldn't?" I said.

"Suppose I reveal it to you. What would be your first wish?" the guy asked.

"I want my science teacher to die," I said.

He laughed loudly and said, "Good you told me before I passed the secret to you. My dear boy, it stops working the minute you wish harm to others. Remember that."

Then he took my open palm into his hand and scribbled something on it while looking up, chanting mantras.

"Now chant this mantra and try to do it yourself," he said.

With some trepidation, I looked up and, chanting the mantra, wrote across my palm with my index finger, "Let there be light."

There was light. It was so bright it looked like day.

"Good. Keep it up," he said.

When I reached the farmhouse, my uncles were shocked as to how I got to the place alone in the dark. The local came forward and told them the story. My uncles thanked the stranger and immediately realized that it was their mistake to have made the journey without waiting for me to return from the science class.

They were struggling to make the dinner with the help of only two naked bulbs to illuminate the farmhouse and the large yard around it. I told them of the secret the stranger passed to me. They didn't believe. They thought I was making excuses for my brashness.

"Come, show us," they said.

"What do you want?" I asked them.

"We want light," they said.

I opened my palm and wrote with my index finger, "Make it day."

At once the entire area around a one-mile diameter was flooded in daylight. The long-distance traffic on the Grand Trunk Road passing through Gunadala stopped to see the wonder. People from neighboring villages like Machavaram and Ramavarappadu came running to witness it as well.

We had a lunch instead of dinner and returned home in the aura of daylight. My uncles advised me to suspend the magic for better use in the future.

When I grew up and became old, say, ninety, I read a Murakami story in which the protagonist kept a blackboard at home on which he would write mainly food items he needed, and the board would deliver them faithfully and instantly.

I remembered this experience of my early school days and wrote this down but always wondered whether what had happened on the road to the farmhouse was real. Meeting a local is not unnatural because it was all farmland on both sides of the road. What strains my credulity even now is whether the yokel could write and materialize whatever he wanted. Nobody takes Murakami's yarn seriously because they know it is all fiction.

On one of my recent visits to Vijayawada, where this farmhouse was, I drove to my grandfather's place. It was not there. A big mall had come up on its ruins. The Muslim burial ground was there but not the tamarind trees or the farmlands. Was my boyhood experience a fiction of my mind, or a dream, or the experience of the transitional state from wakefulness to sleep?

MOTOR CRAZE

My father and his younger brother never drove. When the driver took his weekly day off, or fell ill, it was our youngest uncle who drove them. All of us, four siblings and I, were car lovers as children. The last car our family owned was a Chrysler convertible. There were hardly ten cars plying on the macadamized roads of Bezwada, our first place of residence at the beginning of the Second World War, abrading their tires on the rough gravel, when Gannon Dunkerley and Co. launched a government project to lay motor-friendly roads, bridges, and underpasses to transform the town into a city.

I guess cars were sparingly used in those days, the early 1900s. My grandfather had in his double garage two of the ten cars paying road taxes. A zamindar, two leading lawyers, and the Deccan Diocese owned the rest of the cars. The Diocese car resembled a bus without doors. After my grandfather's death, both our cars also died of disuse.

The most popular brands were Chevrolet and Ford. We owned a convertible Chevrolet and a strange automobile freak called Citroen. Strange because it had solid tires and so never needed replacement. Instead of a shaft, a chain connected the engine to the rear wheels. It had two battery-powered headlamps on either side of the radiator besides two small kerosene lamps flanking the windscreen. We rarely took it out. Sometimes a visitor to the town would drive in a brand that set us guessing because we did not know any brand other than Chevrolet and Ford. One day we sighted a Ford V8 and an Opel, the first sedans we identified with the help of an uncle. That was on the eve of our migration to Hyderabad.

A feast for our eyes awaited us at Hyderabad, celebrating Prime Minister Mirza Ismail's magic touch. It was a challenge to our skills of automobile brand identification. The Nizam, the world's richest man at that time, maintained a vast collection of foreign cars (the Landmaster was a long way off at that time). The Nizam himself had a canvas-topped black Ford Tourer, supreme symbol of his extreme frugality. It was a cousin to our Chrysler convertible. Traffic policemen sometimes mistook our car for Ala Hazrat's car and honored our car with a stiff salute.

In our reckoning, the Nizam's collection began with the seventh Nizam, Mir Osman Ali Khan, acquiring a 1912 Rolls-Royce Silver Ghost, thus ushering in an automobile royalty headed by a triumvirate of Rolls-Royce, Daimler, and Bentley. He acquired it for ceremonial purposes for which horse-drawn carriages had been used earlier. To the automobile proletariat belonged Austen, Wolsley, Opel, and so on. The Nizam never used any one of these cars, which were meant for the Ameira department (hospitality) for use by nondignitaries.

Almost all the cars at that time had hand gears, except a few American cars. We were very eager to be seen driving a car with steering gears. A neighbor of ours took fancy to us and permitted us to drive his Willy's Overland Jeep station wagon. We had an uncle who permitted us to use a Humber car and a jeep acquired in army auctions. When his own Austin arrived, we would drive it whenever he didn't. It was such a junk heap that we never felt we were driving an automobile.

Every year, we had our Chrysler repaired in one of those garages in Siddiambar Bazaar for one hundred rupees. But our main mechanic was our elder brother. In those days, motor engines were simple contraptions. Usually the problem would be with either the carburetor or the battery. He would take out the carburetor and clean it in kerosene oil. He would scratch the battery for life. We would always keep a long wire in the car in case the battery died. We would flag down another car and use the wire to connect the two batteries. When our engine came to life, someone sitting at the wheel would rev it for a few minutes, and we were on our way again. The car had a self-starter, which we never used for fear of weakening the battery. We had a Z-shaped handle that we would insert in an aperture below the bonnet and crank it clockwise until the engine roared.

Petrol was dirt cheap at Rs. 1.14 a gallon. Our father allowed all of us, except the last brother, who was too young, to steer the wheel. Since there was no photograph of the driver pasted on the license in those days, we used a single license for all of us. We were never caught. The trick was to avoid the road where the traffic staff checked licenses. We frequently took out the car, filled it with friends, and drove to the university campus in the evening or sometimes on a full moon night.

It might be an accident that we never had an accident except once. An enterprising Englishman had come to town with a small plane, offering an aerial round of the town for fifty rupees. My mother, chaperoned by the family cook, drove to the airfield and enjoyed the ride. On the way back, the right front wheel separated itself from the car and fled into the roadside fields. The driver chased it down, and there was no harm done.

Our motor craze might've been due to my father's frequent change of cars. A Wolsley was first, which he supplemented with a Ford. A Chevrolet followed. The last car he ever owned was Chrysler, just before a paralytic stroke felled him and erased a thriving career.

CONFESSIONS OF
A WRITER

READING A STORY

I'm reading this story as usual with a bowl full of cashew nuts by my side. It is a story by Saleem, whom I've known for a long time. "Okay. Why nuts?" the reader may ask. The nuts are an essential part of my reading process. The nuts I have by my side came from the cashew plantations of Chirala, not far from where Saleem was born and went to school. These nuts have a history like any institution or individual. They are fruits of research done at the Central Cashew Research Station at Bapatla, a couple of miles from Chirala. "Why not Kerala nuts?" you may ask. The answer is awfully simple. That is because the Chirala nuts are children of the soil. Priyanka is the name of their variety. The name is purely a matter of personal choice. Nothing to do with dynastic politics.

Before I begin reading, it is my habit to count the number of nuts, without caring with what hand. The central idea is to know the statistical relationship between the story and the number of nuts it takes to appreciate it. This is an entirely new approach to literary appreciation. At get, set, go were 122 of them. I don't remember how many nuts an earlier story of Chaya Devi, *Prayanam,* had taken. At that time, I'd not conceived this revolutionary formula for sizing up a short story. I remembered their Brazilian parentage and wondered how effortlessly they had prospered on the hospitable Indian soil.

Yes, I've just started reading the Saleem story with a nut count of 122. The nuts are all washed and look enticing like white, pudgy crescents. "Come. What's the delay?" they seem to taunt me. "Wait, your turn will come," I tell the fatsos. Saleem's story sounds familiar. I remember I translated it a long time ago. So, it shouldn't surprise me that it is familiar. And it makes me happy to know my memory is not poor and my mind is sharp at ninety. Or is it eighty-seven? I'm standing now at the doorstep of the story where I'm swept by a fancy to test my memory more scientifically than by relying on self-assurance. I close my eyes and try to summon the author's name. Syed Saleem! The moniker drops behind my limpid eyelids. "Great!" I shout in celebration and dip two fingers, the thumb and the index finger, into the cashew bowl made of porcelain my wife and I bought from a migrant Rajasthani woman on the footpath opposite Indira Park. She was pretty, but with my wife by my side, I pretended I had no interest. As a tribute to her rural beauty, however, I desisted from haggling over the price.

Yes, the fingers I mentioned in the previous paragraph catch a couple of nuts, the same nuts that looked like pudgy crescents, and catapult the Chirala stuff into my open mouth, which I kept unshut, lest in a moment of abstraction I fail to suck the cashews into my system. No, no. I'm sorry. The truth is I opened my mouth in awe at the grandeur of the lyrical sculpture of the doorstep to the story. Saleem's story titled *Talaq* opens with a theater-crazy Ibrahim winning the hand of a fairy, without wings, in one of his travels with an itinerant repertory. What is the name of the girl? I make a guess. It is Jameelunnisa. I make sure there is no one in the room besides me. But why guess when I can check the anthology in which the story appears? I confirm the name; it is Jameelunnisa. I like the name and regret I didn't give it to my daughter, whose name is Lakshmi Kameswari Siva Prasanna. I don't know how my thoughts have entered the mind of Jameelunnisa. She shouts from line two of page forty, where she appears in the story for the first time, "No, you can't steal the name Saleem Saab has given me." I could've silenced her by just closing the book. No, that would dent my democratic image. So, I tell her we'll talk to Saleem about the name.

Now, let's put this brawl on hold and go back to the story and see what happened. Unable to bear the separation from footloose Ibrahim, the wingless fairy Jameelunnisa joins the repertory so she can be by her husband's side always. In one of Ibrahim's plays being staged that day at Tenali, she and her husband play man and wife. Their names are Hamid and Akhtarunnissa on stage. That they are already man and wife in real life makes things easy for them. Things now begin to happen. Saleem makes them happen in such a manner that Hamid suspects the fidelity of his wife Akhtarunnissa. So, on the stage, Hamid, (Ibrahim in real life), says *talaak* three times in a row and divorces Akhtarunnissa (Jameelunnisa in real life). A *kazi* (a Muslim priest who presides over marriages) sitting in the audience stands up and shouts that the talaak is final even if the words were part of make-believe, and Ibrahim and Jameelunnisa can't live together even on the stage because their marriage is annulled. The fairy girl begins to cry bitterly.

This scene pains me. I go to the green room behind and whisper to her to tell the kazi to go to hell. Then I hear a sudden explosion like the one you see at quarries. From out of the smoke of the explosion appears Saleem, alerted by a premonition. He has this power to appear whenever his texts are in danger of being messed up. God granted him this boon in a previous birth, and it has stayed. He is very agitated, suspecting I'm trying to change his plot.

"Yes, Saleem, what can I do for you?" I ask him with a straight face.

"You've done whatever damage you could already, sir," he says with suppressed anger.

"This is a serious charge. Let's be clear about it," I say to him, trying to show outrage at his incrimination.

"Cool down and tell me what the matter is." I try to pacify him.

He's so worked up he doesn't see me check how many nuts are remaining at this stage of the story in the bowl. Not a single nut. There are only two men in the green room now, Saleem and I. I don't know where the girl has gone. My eyes transmit my suspicion about the missing nuts to Saleem. Alerted by his sharp antennae, he, winner of the Sahitya Akademi award, is less than amused.

"It's an affront to the one-hundred-year-old Telugu short story," he bawls at me.

"But the Telugu short story has not taken off in true sense," I remind him.

"What do you mean?" he says.

"It's still stranded in its infancy by the controversy about who wrote the first Telugu short story," I tell him.

"It's Gurazada who wrote the first story," Saleem says, punching his fist in the air.

"Kondaveeti Satyavati says it's Bandaru Achamamba's *Dhana Trayodasi.*"

"No, it doesn't have the basic ingredients of a short story." Saleem dismisses me.

Saleem is in the middle of his defense of Gurazada when Jameelunnisa rushes into the green room from wherever she's gone. She begins ranting at Saleem at inventing Maulvis and Moulanas to wreck her marriage.

"What can be done now?" I ask Saleem.

"Simple, sir. I'll rewrite the story in consultation with Jameelunnisa," he says.

"In that case, I won't read it," I tell him. Angry, Saleem disappears into an implosion he has triggered. I look piteously into the empty porcelain bowl in which I see the pretty face of the Rajasthani woman and sigh. Next time, I will try to read without the distractions of nuts and a bowl purchased from a Rajasthani woman, I decide.

STRANGERS, SORT OF

There was a time when I described myself as a pretender. That hour called for modesty. So I remained one for so long I came to believe I was one. Now, I have run out of ideas, plots, twists, flashbacks, climaxes, and endings. I have tried to burgle them from the troves of Carver, Cheever, Murakami, even James Joyce, Virginia Woolf, and Nadine Godimer. I first experimented with style. Minimalist, for example. I began dropping adjectives and adverbs. The sentences looked and sounded like skeletons in a medical college.

Okay, let me lift a situation from Cheever. I very soon find it doesn't have a parallel in the Indian landscape. How do I pave the streets of Mumbai with New York's snow? Mumbaikar will look like a joker in the kind of clothes Cheever drapes his characters in. My head became so overheated with ideas of larceny that I ran to take a shower. In the middle of the shower, an epiphany of the Joycean kind struck me.

How did I forget I have a friend in Vijayawada who lives with her husband in an apartment in a leafy suburb? She is a front-rank storyteller in Telugu, a language spoken in India by eighty million people. "So what?" you may ask. All kinds of characters, from maidservants to supermoms, inhabit her short story collections. In my prototype of plagiarism, I imported a truant maidservant and a struggling supermom from one of her stories and wrote an aftermath to the parent story.

I showed it to her. "This is my story," she cried.

"No, madam," I said. "Servant maids and supermoms are everywhere. They can't be patented like you patent your husband. The idea to write an aftermath to your story is mine, exclusively mine. It is something like *Uttara Ramayana*," I said. She laughed. I left her laughing, afraid she might change her mind if I lingered long.

The story haunts me; strictly speaking, it is not a story. In fact, it is about to become one. It has no conclusion, an essential part of a story. It is like a lidless and bottomless receptacle. But the latest literary charivari argues that a story need not have an ending. I would have taken this route, but the story is about a friendship that is on the verge of fruition. I thought, rather concluded, I could never write the finish in a cold climate in the northeast battered by cyclones named after women generally to sound less harsh. Cold weather brings to my mind a Nancy Mitford title of long ago, *Love in a Cold Climate*. So I took off for the warmer southwest Pacific coast by an eight-hour flight.

Friends thought I was running away from the story that needed an ending. But they didn't know the story also was pursuing me southwest, helping me give the lie to the rumor of jettisoning the story. Here is the story beginning as an awkward daily exercise in deflections between two strangers.

We were strangers familiar to each other, familiar because we worked under the same false ceiling, for the same tight-fisted media-owning slave driver. Yet not a word passed between us, not even a smile of knowingness, for the four years we knew each other. This charade remained undisturbed, a relationship so amorphous it eludes definition. Wait, I remember an occasion when we entered the same aisle from opposite ends and found ourselves blocking each other's way. She blushed, and I smiled and pressed myself against the flank of the aisle to let her pass. This short break of exchanging smiles of recognition disappeared when she suddenly stopped reporting for work. No clue about where she went. Even if one were available, what do I do with that info? *Stop thinking about it, you cad,* my inner voice chided me. The reason could be matrimony or maternity. I couldn't think of any other reason for an answer. Were there other possibilities I hadn't explored? *Why don't you check with any one of her colleagues?* something inside me prodded. "Why are you interested?" they might ask me. If that happened, I had nowhere to hide my face. For two months, her absence bothered me like a mote in the eye, like the stain on the wall that tormented Virginia Woolf. This familiar stranger always wore cotton saris, not Woolf, in pastel shades, elegantly pleated down, crisp and starched. She would tilt her head a whit backward, jutting her chin forward. I would look at the glass door she would open at ten every morning, take four steps, turn left, negotiate the alley between the back of my chair and the editor's cabin, and enter her office separated from ours by a weather-bloated plywood partition and vaporize.

When she failed to turn up for work for more than ten days, I ventured to ask an orderly in her office. "You don't know, sir? She is now a lecturer; she has quit," he said. Slowly I got used to the void she created. When I too had to leave the company after five years, she hardly beeped on my radar.

After both of us had left the slave driver's company, a lot of personal and general history happened in the five continents and space. The rivers of the world had emptied trillions of cusecs of water into the oceans in the years that passed as fast as digits in a tampered auto meter. I had lost my parents, three brothers, a sister, and wife. A daughter she gave me went to school and college and settled in the US. Bereaved, I migrated to the States to stay with my daughter. I had spent a voluntary twenty-year exile in Delhi. I was in and out of jobs. South Africa became free. The Soviet empire broke up. We put Rakesh Sharma in space, from where he told Indira Gandhi, "Saare jahan se achcha Hindustan Hamara." Indira Gandhi punctured male and media egos by declaring an emergency. The internet age also dawned.

So much history wrote itself before the familiar stranger weakly beeped on my radar. An email came from her asking me whether I remembered her. I wondered how she got my email. I told her I remembered her well and provided information to assure I remembered her well. A year later, she was in the US and called me. Again, I didn't know how she got my US telephone number. She had come to spend time with her children, who had made the US their home. I don't remember what transpired between us, but those two or three calls helped us to become less of strangers.

I began filling my days in the US translating Indian stories into English and publishing them in a net magazine my daughter and I ran. In the meanwhile, we got to know that the stranger had become one of the top storytellers in her country. We sought permission to translate and publish one of her stories in our magazine. When we completed publishing one hundred stories from our magazine as an anthology, we included in our collection one of her stories too. Mail by mail, we were able to transform our familiarity into friendship.

But the trigger came when, on a visit to my cousin's place, I was told that the stranger lived in that colony in a street next to my cousin's.

I called on her and found that her husband was for a short period our colleague. It was not a useful meeting because the batteries in my hearing aid conked. I went back and wrote a very unconventional report of our dumb colloquy. It appeared as an article with a big picture of hers in a leading newspaper. When she saw it the next morning, she was overwhelmed and shared her joy with her friends. Now, I am known to her friends I don't know personally.

More mail flowed from each side, she telling me about her husband's health, truancy of her servant maid (more about this maid later), and the battle of life, and I writing about my articles, published and rejected. A few mails later, the flow stopped abruptly like water from a municipal tap. A couple of my mails remained unreturned like Martina Hingis's aces.

"Friendship" is a gender-neutral noun just like "they" is a gender-neutral pronoun. Neither of us imagined that fiction would build bridges between us. I saw in her stories an exposition born out of experience. A language that opened a dialogue with the reader. Her pen dipped in conviction and missionary zeal abjured highfalutin and mawkish outpourings.

But how does the story end? Why should it? Chekov, Hemingway, Virginia Woolf, and Raymond Carver have all rejected traditional endings. Each story is part of a greater story that is still in present tense. The story does not get an ending because it would end a friendship.

Now it is for readers to wait for my collection of stories based on ideas I don't own, like you have waited for Arundhati Roy's second title. No, you need not wait for twenty years. My first plagiarized collection in the country will be upon you suddenly like an epiphany.

WRITER'S MAID

Breaking the series of short appearances and long disappearances, my friend and feminist writer Saraswati awakens her computer one morning and asks it to send me a mail telling me she will release her new collection of stories at Vijayawada and wonders whether we could meet there. I saw in the mail a welcome journey for me to the place of my birth, my school, my college, and my work. Also to meet Razia Sultana, her maid servant about whom she talks so effusively, sometimes complainingly too, in every call she makes. Despite Saraswati's talent of vanishing without notice, she and I have always managed to meet before we become memories to each other. Old wine in new bottles, she tells me later about her anthology.

On the day of book release, I go to look her up at the venue, an auditorium for modest gatherings. At the gate, a huge billboard bearing the title page of the book greets me. I enter the hall, shrinking myself to elude notice, and press into an old creaking chair in the third row. Before I can resume my unabridged self, a few old faces manage to relay their recognition to me. The two halves of the curtain on the stage disappear into the wings, rescuing me from the prospect of facing inane inquiries from the crowd that spotted me on arrival a while ago. On the dais, I see ten chairs anxious to be occupied; some of them beam at large in anticipation of impending occupation.

Ten chairs means ten speakers, I guess from experience of attending functions like these organized to present awards, to merely honor a celebrity, to observe anniversaries of writers who are no more, to release a book or an album, and so on. Soon, the ten celebrities and the author will line up on the stage as if they are facing the firing squad, each holding a free copy of the book at waist level, the title page facing the audience. From the well of the stage, paparazzi work their cameras to shower lightning on them for a split second. Unless otherwise ordained, things generally happen this way after the curtains are drawn into the wings: From one wing of the stage, a tallish person in culturally appropriate ethnic habiliment emerges wearing a sense of self-importance on his face, flashing pearls of sweat. He carries a sheaf of papers in his hand and heads directly for the mike as if programmed, taps on the head of the mike, and says hello to nobody in particular. He bends a bit forward to the level of the mouthpiece, clears his throat, and gears himself to invite the ten chair fillers, one by one, to come on to the dais and take their seats.

"I invite Varalakshamma Garu to come on to the dais and grace her seat," the man who wields the mike for the while says. Varalakshamma Garu, past seventy-five, liberates herself from the bug-infested chair in the auditorium and shambles up to the stage, escorted by a girl. The man at the mike says, "Kumari Vimala will now garland Varalakshamma Garu." Vimala comes running up to where the invitee is sitting and realizes she forgot to get the garland. It is now opportunity for another Kumari to sparkle on the stage for a second. By the time the last woman pours herself into the tenth chair on the stage, an hour of spontaneous, though vacuous, pantomime will have played itself out.

Since I am familiar with the tiring rigmarole that will follow on such occasions, I leave the place but with plans of coming back. Ultimately, I return as the sun disappears into the west as a matter of habit. Thank God, the function is over. With the help of an attractive woman volunteer, I find Saraswati in a green room–like enclosure, flopped in a chair, all drained and too weak to eject a word. I go out and get her a warm, cool drink.

Trying to tell me how tired she is, Saraswati merely spreads on her lips a short-lived smile replete with apology. She is wrapped in a crisp white cotton saree, with a thin black border. She looks thinner than when I saw her a year before. She waits for life to flow back into her spare frame and gives me a copy of her just-released anthology, damp with the sweat of her palm. As she swallows the tepid drink drop by drop, I run through the pages and stop at a story titled "The Ant." What could anybody write about an ant? Pinheads. If they are worker ants, they are all female. No love story is possible without a male ant. I chuckle at my sense of humor.

Seeing the smile on my face, Saraswati asks me, "What makes you laugh?" Before I ask her stupid questions like what prompted her to write, I try to get her into a lighter mood.

"So, it is about women's problems. No men, like in the world of ants? How is Pawan? And how is your tormentor, Razia?"

"That's a long story. I told her you are coming to interview her. She is the heroine of 'The Ant' story."

"Oh, it's great fun. Thank you," I tell her.

Common to Saraswati and me is Vijayawada, where we sweated for the same boss for several years. After night shift, we would stop at the Ravindra Cool Drinks watering hole on Besant Road, overrun by relentless twenty-four-hour traffic, half of it consisting of sleepwalkers. Sometimes, we stopped at Matha Café on Eluru Road to be the first customers. Passengers, waiters call them.

We get into Saraswati's chauffeur-driven car and sit in the back seat. The crush of traffic is so suffocating on the road that the car is proceeding as if it were reliving some previous birth as a snail.

Returning after several years, I find that time has erased the city's every landmark that guided out-of-towners. It now looks as if it has been where Siva did his dance of destruction, tattering its original middle-class blueprint. I struggle to guess where we are, though we are passing through the well-known Eluru Road, now known as Mahatma Gandhi Road. This part of the young city never sleeps. Like ants. With great difficulty, I find Dasu Vaari Veedhi (the Street of the Dasus), named after our family off the interstate artery.

The driver suddenly gets animated and asks me excitedly, "Sir, do you belong to Vijayawada?"

"Yes, I was born here, went to college, and worked here."

"Sir, I am so happy to know both of us belong to the same place. What a place, sir!" He goes into a trance, leaving the car in the care of God.

We pass the Muslim burial ground that now hides behind a row of giant billboards. From there, the road looks bare and brown, brick and mortar. Some trees are still there blighted and looking lost. My college and the Anjaneyaswami temple are on the same road. Last time I came here to see Saraswati, I met the principal and told him he was not born when I was a student in that college. Now there is a front garden and a lot of vegetation that has taken away the sting of the temperature. From the college corridor, I could see the giant cross the missionaries had planted on top of the granite hills of the eastern range and the spire of the Virgin Mary temple that wasn't there when I was a student. The place continues to be known as Machavaram.

Saraswati lives in a large building off the Grand Trunk Road, the same I referred to mistakenly as Mahatma Gandhi Road and Eluru Road. The car stops before a three-storied apartment complex. The woman inside the GPS cries in a girlish voice, "You have arrived." The images of the city follow me like a foreboding as we go up in a cage-like elevator to the third floor. Hearing the footsteps in the corridor, Saraswati's husband, Pawan, comes to the front door, smiles, and says, "Welcome." Her husband too was my colleague once.

As we walk in and settle ourselves in a sofa, a young girl enters the hall and smiles at me with her jasmine-white teeth. She is tall with a brownish complexion.

"Razia Sultana alias Varaalu, heroine of the story you read at the book release," Saraswati introduces the girl to me. Razia finds it hard to stop giggling.

"Your Amma Garu told me everything about you," I tell her.

"Amma Garu is an angel," she says and pads into the kitchen, perhaps to make tea for us.

"Pawan, do you remember any of your colleagues at the office?" I ask him.

"Not really. I heard a lot about you only after she found you on the net."

"How are your children in the US?" I ask him.

"They are all okay and keep visiting us by turns. My youngest son will be here in a week," he says. Tea comes in the crowded company of some biscuits.

"How do you spend time, Pawan?" I ask him, blowing on my tea.

"There are books. Some of them written by her. There is the TV with a hundred channels. Most of the time, I talk to her about her stories," he says, looking at her fondly. "I listen to a lot of music."

Tea over, Razia Sultana comes and collects the tea things. I tell her we will begin the interview any time now.

"What should I call you, Razia or Varaalu?"

"Varaalu, sir. Only Amma can call me Razia." Her Amma nicknamed her Razia Sultan after the first and only female ruler of the Delhi Sultanate, known equally for her efficient reign as well as poetry.

"You have kids?"

"Yes. Two, a girl and a boy."

"What does your husband do?"

"Don't ask me," she says with some heat. "He is a bum. He sleeps around."

"How do you manage then?"

"I must live for the sake of my kids. Yet a bit of me dies every day."

"Have you thought of divorce?"

"Sir, you don't know our society. There are too many wolves prowling around to prey on women like me."

"You know so much about the ways of the world. Yet you have small quarrels and arguments with your angel?"

She blushes and bends her head to express her sense of shame. "They're the spice of life, sir. Still, Amma is an angel. But I feel that rich and powerful women like Amma should join with women like me to fight these wolves. Because they attack all women, not just poor ones like me. I am sorry, sir. I have said big words."

"No, no, not at all. But do you read your Amma's stories?"

"Why do you ask me, sir?"

"Because you sound very much like your Amma."

"She honors me by reading them out to me."

"What strikes you most in her writing?"

"Those are big questions for a servant maid, sir. I like her stories because they are not just about memsahibs but also about poor women like me. I like that she asks me about how I live and the problems I face every day, and takes the trouble to write about them."

Saraswati's jaw drops. Mine too. I remember Gray's lines:

Full many a gem of the purest ray serene

The Dark unfathomed caves of the ocean bear.

I look at my watch and find it is time to leave. "Thank you, Razia. Happy meeting you."

"Thank you, sir. It is my pleasure," she says.

"Okay, guys, see you again. Let me tell you. Razia is amazing."

BUSTING STEREOTYPES

I'd attained the age of an Indian voter a month before millions of believers born and raised in India declared allegiance to Pakistan, a swath of India for ages. Soon its citizens became them, different from us. Later, both countries went to war with each other three times in ten years. We soon created stereotypes of each other, the om symbol for the Hindus, the crescent for the Muslims, green for the Muslims and saffron for the Hindus, and also invented obscenities to define each other. This is the background for the story you are reading now.

That day, the weeklong UN-sponsored deliberations on Namibia ended at the Guyanese capital of Georgetown. The sun was calling it a day when the delegates trooped out of the conference hall of Hotel Pegasus with its stunning view of the Atlantic. They shook hands of farewell, took out their ballpoint pens from their jackets, and jotted down one another's addresses and telephone numbers. They had all met years ahead of the mobile phone and the internet. Then they went back to their rooms to pack their bags for different destinations and, time permitting, to do some hurried shopping. The UN office had booked me for a night flight that day.

It was five in the evening when a UN official knocked on the door of each delegate to the conference to make payments. According to UN rules, part of the payment would be in local money, the Guyanese currency. We were paid US$1,500 and several thousands in local currency. The official took our signatures to acknowledge receipt of money. Since the Guyanese currency was not convertible, we'd spend it in Georgetown itself in less than three hours. In fact, it was one hour only because shops in Guyana closed early. I took a taxi and went downtown. I thought if I went for a gold chain, it was easy to carry, and I would get rid of the local currency. I couldn't find a single shop that sold twenty-two-carat gold. It was fourteen-carat everywhere. On a previous foreign trip, I had brought home a fourteen-carat gold chain. My wife was not very happy. So, this time I bought two Caribbean shirts, two watches, Casio and Q&Q, for me and for my wife. I was left with a few hundred Guyanese dollars. I kept fifty for the airport tax and gave away the rest to the hotel waiters.

A UN van brought us to the airport for the 9:00 p.m. flight to JFK. Delegates from New York took that flight. They checked in, went through immigration and customs, and boarded the Guyanese Airways plane. When the belt sign went up, I fastened my seat belt and felt happy to be returning home. It was then I found the face of my neighbor at the window seat familiar. I remembered he'd chaired one of the sessions I spoke at, a delegate from Pakistan. We had not started a conversation when the drink cart rolled in. It didn't interest me. I was worried about how I could reach the Sloan House YMCA hostel in Manhattan. I was warned that most cabbies in New York were immigrants from India, Pakistan, and Bangladesh and were likely to take first-time visitors for a metered ride. *Okay, let us tackle it when the moment comes*, I thought.

I don't remember who broke the ice, but the Pakistani delegate and I got talking. He was a diplomat attached to the Pakistani consulate in New York. I told him I was a journalist back home in India. I found him a handsome and extremely polite person in a navy blue suit. He told me his parents had migrated from Uttar Pradesh to Pakistan following partition of the country in 1947.

"That is interesting. Where in Uttar Pradesh?" I asked him.

"Lucknow," he said.

"That's great. I come from Hyderabad," I said.

"Two great centers of Urdu," he said.

"Do you remember your days in India?" I asked him.

"Not really. I remember my school in a vague way. We've relatives in Hyderabad," he said.

"That's natural," I said.

"The visas are a problem. There are too many restrictions, too much red tape," he said.

"I understand. It is the climate of distrust."

"When will we get out of it?"

"Distrust is the engine driving politics and politicians. Just as every eminent doctor builds his reputation on the number of well-known persons he'd dispatched to the nether world, politicians get into history books for the riots they're able to engineer."

The diplomat took my hand, shook it, and said, "Well said, sir. Shall I call for a drink?"

"No, sir, thank you."

"How do you think the two countries can work for better ties?" he asked me.

"They've reached a low mainly because of politicians and the media on both sides. Hatred has more takers than love. Politicians play on the emotions of the people to become popular. The media exaggerate differences. Both countries should ignore the two wreckers of détente," I said.

"That's right, I believe. We have our own problems like the alternation of civilian and army rule. It is commonsense that peace between the two countries brings down the expenditure on defense," the diplomat said.

He asked me my destination. New York, I said and disclosed to him my apprehension about the cabbies.

"Where are you staying in New York?" he asked me.

"Manhattan," I said.

"Don't worry. The embassy car will pick me up at JFK. I will drop you at YMCA."

The food cart was wheeled in. I picked up the vegetarian tray, and the diplomat the nonvegetarian tray. The food smelled of garlic. I just took the yogurt and dessert and waited for the drink cart to come a second time. The food in my tray brought back memories of my experience in the city I'd left a few hours ago. On the first day of my stay in Hotel Pegasus, I'd visited its restaurant and found nothing I could relish. I called for a couple of sandwiches and rounded them off with fruit juice. On the second day, I took a taxi and went looking for Indian restaurants. The taxi took me to at least twenty restaurants. None served vegetarian food. I thought with 40 percent of the population being Indian in origin, there would be some vegetarian restaurant somewhere. So, at the hotel restaurant, I called daily for sandwiches and fruit juice. It intrigued the waiter, who looked at me with some amusement.

It reminded me of another vegetarian embarrassment. It happened in Mosul in Iraq. All journalists covering the Iraqi general election in 1980 were invited to a state dinner. Each table was set for four persons. After a short while, the service began. A waiter brought a huge platter full of biryani with a whole lamb stuffed with a variety of spicy ingredients. The three others at the table were Arab journalists who did not know English. If I walked away, it would offend the Arabs. Luckily, the waiter placed a bowl of grapes too. I began helping myself to some grapes. The Arab facing me asked in sign language why I was not eating. I replied in the same sign language that I was not well. Poor guy tried to be nice to me by offering grapes to me with the hand that he'd dipped in the biryani. I shammed stomachache and went out and bought some biscuits and ate them right at the shop. I waited outside for my colleague to finish lunch and come out. Fortunately, we found at our Baghdad hotel an Egyptian waiter who knew how to make vegetarian food. So daily we had dal, *chaval,* and okra *sabji.*

At JFK, the immigration cleared my neighbor on the airplane on a priority basis because of his diplomatic status. An hour later, I emerged from the immigration and found to my surprise that he was waiting for me. I thanked him. We drove to YMCA. I got out, and when the chauffeur opened the trunk, I reached to collect my bags. No, sir, the diplomat said, and told his chauffeur to put my bags in the foyer of the Sloan House. He shook my hand, waved a goodbye, and drove away.

Now, another story was waiting to happen at the registration window. To my shock, the YMCA man at the counter told me that there had been no UN request to reserve a room for me. I'd to join a long line of accommodation seekers. Ahead of me in the line stood a person with Indian features. I told him my problem. He told me not to worry. I could share his room, he said. Meanwhile, a YMCA official walked up to me and asked me my problem. I said without a room I would be roofless in a new place. "Wait for half an hour. I will get you one," the official told me. I heaved a sigh of relief and went to the person who offered to share his room with me to thank him. I spoke in Hindi to him, and he responded in Hindi to me. I asked him where in India he lived. He told me he was from Bangladesh! All that hatred we are taught to carry with us cannot overcome our humanity.

A MEMORABLE
ROAD TRIP

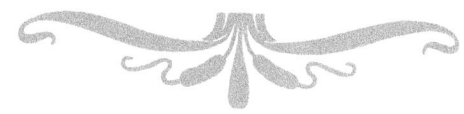

The American Experience

The first person who introduced America to me was a person called Washington Irving. In his short story *Rip Van Winkle,* he described a swathe of the Catskill mountain range not far from New York. Even earlier, Hollywood films showed us snow-bound streets of New York, its T-model Fords and horse-drawn streetcars. My early visits to the USA with my wife were filled with the wonder of discovery of a vast new continent and the delight of new grandparenthood.

My wife and I first came to the United States, as most Indian parents do, to help our expectant daughter. After a month of hectic preparation—What should we pack? What should we take for the expecting parents? What about the grandchild?—we landed at JFK on a midwinter evening threatening to become night. In the excitement of arrival, we forgot to shiver in the killing cold of New York. That arrival is now a distant memory.

As newcomers, we blindly joined the caravan of passengers rushing through the airport corridors toward immigration halls to be ahead of others in the lines forming before immigration counters. On the way, we could see the dying relics of Christmas revelry of a few days ago. From the immigration line, my wife noticed a six-year-old boy crying for his mother, who had gone to use the washroom. "What kind of a woman leaves a child alone in a strange new place?" she muttered. As our turn came, the immigration man mechanically stamped our passports and, to our delight, opened a flash conversation on Ravi Shankar.

We collected our bags from the belts, and as we headed for the exit gate past the customs, Kumar, my son-in-law, spotted us from outside the exit gate and waved to us. When we came out, he handed each one of us a can of Sprite. "How was the journey?" he asked us. Tired, we merely mumbled okay and sat silently through the drive to his flat in Newport (Jersey City) across the Hudson. My daughter opened the door. The first thing we did on stepping in was to present a Conjeevaram saree to her, complying with a tradition. After a meal, we fell into a dark, unconscious sleep.

Next morning, we awoke to an American sun and surprises. We plugged in the coffeemaker and pushed up (not down as we do in India) the switch to get it going. My son-in-law had already left for work. My wife was glued to the large window of the twenty-third-floor apartment, unable to turn away from the World Trade Center towers presiding over a frozen Hudson River, gleaming golden in the early morning sun. That window became her addiction. She'd point out a passing cruise ship to me or call out the firework displays over the river. Knowing her delivery was only thirteen days away, my daughter was anxious that we do a bit of sightseeing. We went down to the lobby in a lift the Americans called elevator. As I was looking at the display to watch the progress of the elevator, I found that there was no thirteenth floor.

Despite our protests, my daughter took us to Battery Park in New York to catch the ferry to the Statue of Liberty. The cabbie sat at the wheel on the left side and drove in the right lane. A Jamaican musician played fragments of the Indian national anthem to entertain us while we waited in line for the ferry. We really did not enjoy the trip to the statue because we worried about premature delivery. The statue seemed to welcome us to discover the beauty of the American landmass and its great lakes, mountain ranges, deserts—and diversity.

Very early on our first visit, we saw, besides the Statue of Liberty, the Empire State Building and went up the 107th floor of the World Trade Center. From its dizzying height, you could get a glimpse of the orthogonal layout of the streets of Manhattan, a type of city plan in which streets run at right angles to each other to form a grid. You could also see the automobiles reduced to the size of insects and the blinking traffic lights of Manhattan. But what excited my wife, a lover of flowers, were the azaleas in bloom in the Brooklyn botanical garden. It reminded her of the rampage of bougainvillea in a university campus near our home in Delhi. Our visits took us to the Bronx botanical gardens as well, the world-famous Strand Book Store, and the Trump Taj Casino in Atlantic City, where we played the slot machines, losing and winning petty sums.

The location of the UN headquarters on New York's soil symbolizes the demographic diversity of New York. It is the world miniaturized. Our erratic visits to the city could hardly capture its bewildering heterogeneity, its art museums, separate havens for artists, writers, social dropouts, its fashion boutiques, its street music, the food carts and its skyscrapers, enclaves of different nationalities like China Town and Flushing, Queens, which is home to the Ganesh temple, one of the oldest Hindu temples in the USA. On one such trip to Jackson Heights, we experienced the notorious American traffic jam, stuck for more than four hours in the middle of the homebound revelers of the Puerto Rican parade.

My wife had always said first on her list of places to visit in the US was the Niagara Falls constantly throwing up rainbows in every drop of water. We returned to the USA a year later for our grandson's first birthday. It was also the time for my daughter to receive her PhD degree at Rochester, New York, where we arrived, touching on our way the same Catskill mountain range Washington Irving had immortalized in his story. From Rochester, we drove to Buffalo, from where we took off to Niagara.

The falls, confluence of three waterfalls, was the main attraction. From the American side, a boat called *Maid of the Mist* took us close to the foot of the falls. All of us wore hooded raincoats available in the boat. The roar of the water was so deafening we couldn't hear each other even while standing face-to-face. The few minutes we stood there facing the intimidating majesty of the falls, we forgot the world we belonged to. The falls is also the venue where David Copperfield demonstrated his illusionist games.

In the summer of 1995, my son-in-law planned an ambitious north-south tour that uncovered for us a considerable part of the continent. In the family album is a picture of my wife and I waiting on the shore of Lake Tahoe for the ferry doing a circular tour of the lake. From the lake, we drove to San Jose, stopping on the way for half an hour at Calistoga in Sacramento to see the hot water springs erupting every fifteen minutes. The temperature there reminded us of a scorching New Delhi summer.

My wife had read in some magazine about President Johnson's wife, Lady Bird's, efforts to make America's highways more aesthetically pleasing by planting trees and shrubs along North County's freeways. On this long north-south trip, she could see the endless ribbon of oleander foliage along Interstate 5. All along the highway from San Francisco to Los Angeles to San Diego, these oleanders dazzled the eye.

From Sacramento, we drove to San Jose, where my cousin's son and daughter took us on an academic pilgrimage of Stanford, Berkeley, and Santa Cruz campuses. We also took off time to see San Francisco and ride its vintage trams, snaking through its crooked and undulating arteries and the Asia Society museum and Fisherman's Cove. Our joy was tempered by a bad experience at the Golden Gate Park, where our son-in-law's camera was stolen along with our return tickets to New York and the house keys. But our spirits recovered as we continued our road trip.

One of the highlights of our tour was the Hearst Castle at San Simeon. History knows William Randolph Hearst as the rival of John Pulitzer in egging on President William McKinley to go to war with Spain. I remember it for an interesting experience my wife had at the foot of the hill on which it was built. We had to climb around two hundred steps to reach the front of the palace. With a leaking valve in her heart, she couldn't do it. Seeing our predicament, a young American tourist simply cradled her in his arms and bounded up the steps to the main palace with apparent ease.

It was a novel experience for my wife and me, the road trip. Checking in and out of hotels, being on the move constantly from Monterey to Pismo Beach to Santa Barbara all the way to San Diego, the complimentary breakfast spread of pancakes, croissants, muffins and hash browns, and the stream of hungry patrons eager to see the wonders of the stunning Californian coast. We saw the Monterey aquarium where our grandson bought a dolphin toy, toured the settings for Steinbeck's stories, and marveled at Clint Eastwood's picture postcard of a town, Carmel-by-the-Sea.

My wife was disappointed by what Disney had to offer, having built up an image that nothing could live up to. Unaware of the seriousness of her heart's weakness, we even went on a roller-coaster ride. The Indian eateries on the way never failed to disappoint in the mediocrity of the fare on offer. This is when my wife developed an addiction to french fries and milkshakes; "Heart be damned," she'd say. At the San Diego Zoo, where our trip culminated, we came upon long lines caused by a malfunctioning computer system. Our grandson bought a collection of animal toys there, which he would arrange in migrating streams across the living room back in New Jersey.

The final American road trip in my wife's company began in the first week of 1999 when we set out to meet my nephew, who lived in College Station where his university, Penn State, was. On the way, we passed through Philadelphia, where we saw the Annenberg School of Journalism and toured the Wharton Business School, of which my son-in-law is an alumnus. We then drove to State College, where my nephew Vikram, his wife, and child lived. He took us for a sail on Lake Perez, popularly known as Stone Valley Lake. He also took us out to a maidan where July 4 fireworks were in progress, set to music.

In Youngstown and Cleveland, all in Ohio, we spent a weekend with our cousins and saw the butterfly museum there. The Youngstown cousin, married to an American woman from the Midwest, hosted us to an authentic, homemade Telugu lunch. He later told us that an enterprising Telugu woman who came to America to make a living had made it. From State College, we drove to the summit of the Penn Hills to visit the famous Venkateswara Temple in Pittsburgh, which looked like a modest offering to the Lord compared to the grandeur of the temple at Bridgewater in New Jersey.

On our tours, we found localism a conspicuous feature of American life, a principle on which the borders of most Indian states were redrawn after independence. But the land is truly beautiful, from sea to shining sea.

After the tour, my wife and I went home carrying the bewitching memories of the country's demographic, geographic, and cultural diversity.

ABOUT THE AUTHOR

Educated at Andhra University, the University of Bombay, and Osmania University, Dasu Krishnamoorty (ninety-three) was an editorialist with the Indian print media between 1948 and 1989. He began with the *Hyderabad Bulletin*, and continued his career with the *Deccan Chronicle*, the *Daily News*, the *Sentinel* (all Hyderabad dailies), the *Indian Express, Vijayawada*, the *Times of India, Ahmedabad*, and finally *Patriot* and *Link, New Delhi*.

He was a senior political commentator with All India Radio's national and domestic services for ten years and taught mass communication at Osmania University (Hyderabad), Indian Institute of Mass Communication (New Delhi), and the University of Hyderabad for eighteen years. After his migration to the United States, he wrote for the internet media for fifteen years. He is now an anthologist (1947 Santoshabad Passenger, Jumma, Harvest Festival) and storyteller.